A DREAM OF KINGS

BOOKS BY HARRY MARK PETRAKIS

Novels

Lion at My Heart
The Odyssey of Kostas Volakis
A Dream of Kings
In the Land of Morning
The Hour of the Bell
Nick the Greek
Days of Vengeance
Ghost of the Sun
Twilight of the Ice
The Orchards of Ithaca
The Shepherds of Shadows

Short Story Collections

Pericles on 31st Street
The Waves of Night
A Petrakis Reader: 27 Stories
Collected Stories
Legends of Glory and Other Stories
Cavafy's Stone and Other Village Tales

Memoirs and Essays

Stelmark: A Family Recollection
Reflections: A Writer's Life, a Writer's Work
Tales of the Heart: Dreams and Memories of a Lifetime
Journal of a Novel
Song of My Life

Biographies/Histories

The Founder's Touch: The Life of Paul Galvin of Motorola
Henry Crown: The Life and Times of the Colonel
Reach Out: The Story of Motorola and its People

A DREAM OF
KINGS

A Novel

HARRY MARK PETRAKIS

New Foreword by Dan Georgakas

The University of South Carolina Press

Published by the University of South Carolina Press
Columbia, South Carolina 29208

www.sc.edu/uscpress

Manufactured in the United States of America

24 23 22 21 20 19 18 17 16 15
10 9 8 7 6 5 4 3 2 1

Library of Congress Cataloging-in-Publication Data
can be found at http://catalog.loc.gov

ISBN 978-1-61117-535-6 (paperback)

For Dr. Sanford (Sandy) Weisblatt,
Dr. Nicholas Vick, and Dr. Peter Economov,
with gratitude and affection

FOREWORD

This new edition of *A Dream of Kings* will introduce the work of a legendary Greek American author to a new generation of readers and, one hopes, will generate renewed scholarly interest in his literary legacy. *A Dream of Kings* was a *New York Times* best-seller and a finalist in the National Book Awards of 1966. It was subsequently translated into a dozen languages and was adapted for a 1969 motion picture starring Anthony Quinn and Irene Papas.

A Dream of Kings, like most of Petrakis's work, is set in a Greek environment. He says he uses the Greek perspective as a stepping stone to reach a setting in which he is comfortable. He believes his Greek focus is not unlike William Faulkner's southern environment or James Joyce's Irish setting.[1] Speaking with critics, he stresses his use of Hellenic culture as a vehicle to write about the human condition and its moments of revelations. "I am not a Chicago writer and I am not a Greek writer. A good writer transcends any one time or place."[2]

Petrakis takes pride in being a storyteller. He states his objective is not to show the complexity of his visions, but to reduce them to essentials: "I am a traditional writer. That is my strength and I don't feel it is a limitation. Storytellers entertain, but they also help us endure the terrors of the night."[3] He took great joy when Isaac Bashevis Singer won the Noble Prize in literature. He felt that in honoring Singer, the Noble Prize committee was honoring all storytellers.[4]

The story told in *A Dream of Kings* is that of the flamboyant Leonidas Matsoukas. His son Stavros suffers from an unnamed, fatal disease that leaves the child speechless, totally helpless, and given to frequent convulsions. Matsoukas believes that if can take his son from Chicago and expose him to the sunlight of Greece, it will be a miraculous cure.

Finding funds to realize his crazed dream of a healing Hellenic sun is not an easy task for Matsoukas. His realm is Chicago's Greektown where he ekes out an income operating the Pindar Counseling Service. His infrequent clients mainly seek advice about sex and real estate. More substantial bursts of cash come from his chronic gambling. His family's well-being, however, ultimately is dependent on income provided by his shrewish mother-in-law who lives with them. In due course, Matsoukas becomes so financially desperate that he violates his own code of ethics and uses loaded dice in an ill-fated attempt to gain the money needed for airfare to Greece.

Matsoukas is a Divine Fool, sometimes insightful, often absurd, always a dramatic presence. He constantly embellishes his discourse with grandiose references to Greek mythology, literature, and history. His colorful phrasing often sounds like English versions of statements that would be more striking in the original Greek. The voice of Petrakis is quite different. Drawing on his own troubled past as a chronic gambler, Petrakis offers realistic accounts of Greektown's betting parlors with sharp sketches of various dealers and gamblers.

Matsoukas seems to have boundless energy and enthusiasm for life, but at one point he tells his son, "We are things of a day. . . . Man is a shadow's dream."[5] Leaving a Greek Orthodox Church, he makes the sign of the cross and states, "Man have mercy on you."[6] Cicero, his dearest friend, believes Matsoukas is a man fated for eternal disasters and endless catastrophes, but also a man who is a high-minded warrior who has never learned to accept boundaries. "You give life an offering of an undivided heart."[7]

Caliope, the wife of Matsoukas, is less generous. She berates him for thinking he breathes a different air than other mortals. She says he has always been a selfish and irresponsible fool. She considers his Greek dream a form of madness.[8] Anthoula, his lover, also ultimately berates him. She tells him if he goes to Greece, she will not wait for him like a hapless Penelope.

The major characters in *A Dream of Kings* all have classical names. The historic Leonidas was the Spartan king in command at the Battle of Thermopylae. Caliope is the name of the wife of Ares, god of war. Anthoula is associated in Greek mythology with blossoms. Cicero bears the name of the Roman senator noted for his republican values. Stavros is a name rooted in the Greek word for the holy cross and Matsoukas refers to him as "the crucified one."[9] Matsoukas's daughters are named Faith and Hope. He expresses love for them, but never gives them serious attention.

Petrakis believes there is irony in giving an ordinary person, even a hot dog vendor, a classical name. "The first reaction is amusement. Yet as we get into the story we see tragedy without the trappings of royalty. The beauty of dealing with Greeks is that the awareness of historic links isn't contrived. I write about the heroic actions of common people."[10]

Petrakis has won a number of literary awards and his fiction has been praised by eminent authors such as John Cheever, Isaac Bashevis Singer, Elie Wiesel, Wright Morris, Kurt Vonnegut Jr., and Mark Van Doren. Nonetheless, his work has received limited scholarly attention. *A Dream of Kings* is quintessential Petrakis, containing most of the literary strategies that have characterized his entire body of work. It would be a good place to initiate a study of a literary legacy that now includes over twenty titles. *A Dream of Kings* remains an exceptional work of fiction from a master storyteller, ready to be discovered anew by contemporary readers.

Dan Georgakas

Notes

1. Dan Georgakas interview with Harry Park Petrakis. In 1982 I conducted a multihour interview with Harry Mark Petrakis. The interview was never published, but it will be donated to the National Hellenic Museum in Chicago. Through the years I have spoken frequently with Petrakis about his work. All quotes attributed to him are from my interview and other comments derive from various follow-up conversations through the years.

2. Interview with Dennis E. Hensley, "Hensley's Book Makers," *Muncie Weekly News*, July 20, 1978

3. Georgakas/Petrakis interview.

4. Ibid.

5. Harry Mark Petrakis, *A Dream of Kings* (New York: St. Martin's Press, 1990), 18. All subsequent references are from this paperback edition.

6. Ibid., 92

7. Ibid., 32.

8. Ibid., 175.

9. Ibid., 92.

10. Georgakas/Petrakis interview.

CHAPTER ONE

Spring of the year. A morning in early April like a knife driven suddenly into the cold strong heart of winter.

His body sprang awake to the cries of birds. They were the seagulls taking flight from his dreams, fleeing the winged ship that carried his soul through the visions of the night. With their departure a truce of daylight lingered across the wine-dark and turbulent waters.

He slid carefully from the bed, edging his big naked body toward the precipice of the lumpy mattress, swinging his legs over the side in an arduous effort not to waken his wife, Caliope. Her body and head were hidden beneath the pillow and disheveled blankets but several long and oily strands of her hair spread like twisted stalks across the pillow.

The head of the Medusa, Matsoukas thought, and then in affectionate atonement he gently stroked the broad outline of her rump. He felt her flesh quiver and respond even in sleep to the caress of his fingers.

In the bathroom, the missing tiles making a checkerboard of the walls, he stood before the cracked vanity mirror that severed his face into jagged halves. He soaped his cheeks vigorously and shaved, tilting his head, contorting his mouth to meet each swift slashing pass of the straight razor that he handled as if it were a saber. He flung the soap and stubble the blade gathered into the stool and swept the razor under a spray of lukewarm water on its return to his face. He finished with a brisk patting of scented lotion to his cheeks and then regarded his reflection with satisfaction.

Despite the distorted visage in the cracked glass, his head appeared hewn from some dark and basaltic rock, his craggy face a ravaged bas-relief from a Greek column. His black hair, giving no hint of his forty-seven years, clustered thickly at his temples. His sharply peaked brows seemed reins haplessly seeking to restrain the wild, dark lunge of his eyes. His broad nose, broken and never properly mended after his match with Zahundos, exhaled into the forest of a roguish moustache that bristled about the ivory stockade of his strong white teeth. The only feature that affronted his vanity were his long and unshapely ears, one a half-inch lower than the other, giving his head a lopsided appearance. In addition both ears had lobes so large they might have provided a pair of smaller ears for a conventional head.

He gathered his clothes and dressed in the damp and dingy kitchen. He slipped into the same shirt he had worn the day before, trying vainly to smooth the wrinkles, sniffing at the armpits, scowling at the frayed collar, feeling it an imposition to be reminded of his economic debilities so early in the day. He looped his tie into a wide knot and pulled it up to clasp his thick and muscle-corded throat.

Ready to leave, he walked quietly down the hall, holding his nose in bitter distaste as he passed his mother-in-law's lair, releasing it only when he came to the room in which his two small daughters slept. He pushed open the door gently and listened until he could hear the whispers of breath that rose from their beds.

He passed down the hall and entered the parlor. Within the bay formed by three high and narrow windows a single child's bed stood, a bed that resembled a cage because of the high bars and railings along the sides.

He stood beside the bed looking down at his sleeping son, Stavros, seeing the boy quiet for a beneficent interlude, undisturbed by the dreadful struggles that consumed him when awake. Yet even in sleep his flesh seemed an almost transparent shell spread tightly over the bone of his cheeks. His breath, coming in short spasms up the frail canal of his throat, fluttered a network of roots around his mouth, twisting his lips in sour little patterns. His whole body bore an affinity to shadow.

Matsoukas looked bitterly at the feeble sun barely visible in the sky. Everything was washed in a strange pallor, the window frame, the roofs of buildings, and the arabesque of the elevated tracks.

He began to speak to his son in a whisper so soft the words barely sounded beyond the edge of his lips.

"The sun has risen but you cannot see or feel it," he said. "It is pale and without strength and beneath it even the weeds wither and die. But soon now, my beloved, we will leave this place of dark and rot, soon you will feel the sun of the old country, the sun of Hellas."

He closed his eyes and felt himself caught in a frenzy of recall.

"You have never seen a sun like that," he whispered. "It warms the flesh, toughens the heart, purifies the blood in its fire. It will make you well, will burn away your weakness with its flame, will heal you with its grace."

He fumbled in his pocket and brought out a small cube of sugar. He peeled off the paper and slipped the cube under the boy's pillow. He kissed the tips of his fingers and placed them softly against his son's moist cheek.

He left the flat, drawing the door closed quietly behind him.

"How are you, Matsoukas?" Toundas, the bartender at the Olympia, asked him uneasily.

"Enough time wasted on the amenities!" Matsoukas said. "A glass of ouzo and a cup of steaming black coffee!"

Toundas, frail and lamb-faced, peered nervously at the closed door beyond the end of the bar. "Your credit has been cut off, you know," he whispered. "It would mean my ass."

"My friend," Matsoukas said gently, "you cannot honestly expect me to fret over the past, present, or future fate of your ass. Just a glass of ouzo and a cup of coffee."

Toundas poured him the coffee with trembling hands. "Don't you have thirty cents to pay for the ouzo?" he pleaded.

"Not a drachma! My income goes to sustain my family and not to fill the fat pockets of scoundrels like your boss."

"I can't!" Toundas closed his eyes. "I can't!"

"You don't seem to understand," Matsoukas said patiently. "My day is just beginning and it is important that it start well. In the course of this day I will bite into ripe sweet fruit, pull the cork from at least one bottle of wine, take the hand of a friend—perhaps your fortunate

4

hand—in a pledge of friendship, read aloud a few of the odes of mighty Pindar, look upon the loveliness of women, (but none, he thought, more lovely than Anthoula) perhaps like Prometheus carry my fire into the thighs of at least one, conduct the rigorous demands of my business under the venerable influence of the stars, and, finally sit down to a plate of pungent moussaka."

At a corner table an early morning drunk sleeping with his head cradled in his arms, snored a sibilant grunt of resignation. Toundas poured a small glass of ouzo and placed it before Matsoukas. He returned the bottle to the shelf and sadly loosened his apron in preparation for his discharge. Matsoukas finished the ouzo and coffee calmly and waved the bartender a fond farewell.

Outside on the street he walked with a long brisk stride that made the blood flow through his arms and legs. He paused before the window of a haberdashery to admire a tie of scarlet-dotted magnificence. He studied his reflection in the glass, adjusted the brim of his hat at a rakish angle, and buttoned the top button of his suitcoat which he wore locked in military style.

He stood at the corner waiting to cross, staring with revulsion at the cars streaming past. He was particularly repelled by the miniature ones in the shape of distended beetles. He braced himself wondering if it might be feasible to let a beetle hit him so he might retain an attorney to sue for bodily injury. The cursed things might be deceiving, however, he had heard they were built like small tanks and he could be seriously maimed. He shrugged and crossed the street.

He entered the Tegea Grocery and breathed with fervent pleasure the sharp aroma of Calamata olives in

5

brine mingled with the scent of mezithra and kaseri cheese. He walked slowly along the counter toward the loaves of cheese. Akragas, the short squat grocer, dark tufts of hair sprouting like the stems of radishes from his ears, stared at him in hostility.

"My esteemed landlord!" Matsoukas rendered Akragas a snappy salute. "Descendant of the great eunuch, Ali Pimp! All commoners genuflect by clutching the left ball in reverence!" He bent low in a mock bow and grabbed at his crotch with a groan. He straightened up quickly. "Enough fooling around," he said somberly. "Have any clients been in asking for me?"

The grocer's lip curled in derision. "Have any mice been in asking for the cat?" he sneered.

Matsoukas started toward the narrow stairway in the rear of the store, pausing to pick up several pieces of his mail from the end of the counter. Akragas delivered a parting salvo.

"I could have rented that office again yesterday to Madame Galapi for piano lessons," he said loudly. "Instead of such a responsible tenant I have a boob like you waiting for customers who rarely show up. I will not wait two months for my rent again! Next time I sign an eviction notice for sure!"

"You would miss me, old sport," Matsoukas said. "Be patient and someday I will write you an epinician ode immortalizing your good humor and your generosity."

Matsoukas heard him grumbling and cursing as he ascended the stairs. He entered a small windowless hall and walked between rough-stuccoed walls from which the old paint had peeled. At the end of the hall, before the dim outline of a glass door, he reached up and caught

6

the dangling cord of the socket. In the first snapping of light he marked with a curse that Akragas had changed the bulb again, substituting one of a smaller wattage. He had to hold the bulb almost against the door to illuminate the lines of black lettering that completely filled the glass. He stood reading each word with the same measured delight he felt each morning, reliving for a zestful moment the years of trial and struggle in which he had nurtured and mastered the listed skills.

PINDAR MASTER COUNSELING SERVICE

Leonidas Matsoukas—President
Doctor of Wisdom and Inspiration
University of Experience
and
College of Life

Palmistry–Astrology–Omen Analysis–
Inspiration to overcome drinking, bed-
wetting, and impotence–Greek poems
written for all occasions–Real Estate
Bought and Sold–Wrestling Instruction
(Hellenic Champion of Pittsburgh 1947-
1948)–Vocabulary Tutoring–Personality
Improvement–Talent Agent for Banzakis
Restaurants (Attractive hostesses in special
demand)

BY APPOINTMENT ONLY

He inserted his key into the lock and after some grunt-ing and pushing, the balky bolt snapped back and the door opened. He stepped into the small office cloaked in heavy shadows. He walked around the desk sure of himself in the dark, and raised the shade of the single

7

large window. He stood staring down at the kitchen door of the bakery across the alley, feeling his heart lunging in a tumultuous sea of his blood.

The bakery belonged to Anthoula (even her name ravaged his flesh) since the death of her husband of a heart attack more than a year before. For these many months Matsoukas had been witness to the somber ritual of her mourning. She rose several hours before daylight (he had once stayed in his office overright to confirm how early her lights went on) and she worked steadily in the bakery until evening, most of her time spent in the kitchen baking the bread and trays of sweets while a tart-tongued old lady named Barboonis waited on trade in the store. Each evening after the bakery closed Anthoula retreated to the small apartment upstairs whose windows faced his window across the alley. After supper she again descended to the kitchen to bake for the following dawn.

In the beginning he had pitied her because she was young, no more than thirty, and her husband had been stricken in his prime. As the months passed and she held rigidly to her mourning, attending church dressed in widow's black on Sunday mornings, Matsoukas felt himself drawn to her for the fierce allegiance she accorded her dead. At the same time he could not help thinking of her lush and lovely body deprived of a man's caresses.

Every so often during the day for most of the year (except in the coldest months of winter) she came fleetingly into the alley from the kitchen to empty some paper or scraps into one of the cans. Dressed to work beside the blazing ovens she wore only a sleeveless white shift and Matsoukas had long decided that she must be naked beneath it. The sight of her bare legs and bare feet in

8

thonged sandals, her shapely bare arms smudged with stains of flour, and her glistening black hair bound into a great bun at the back of her head filled him with a wild fluting of desire.

Yet for all of his longing he had never managed to speak more than a dozen words to her at a time. She rarely emerged from the kitchen. On those infrequent occasions when the trade became too much for old lady Barboonis to handle and she pressed the buzzer by the register that rang in the kitchen, Anthoula came out to wait swiftly on customers and quickly return to her sanctuary. Still Matsoukas knew that Anthoula felt his muted desire. On a number of instances he had turned and caught her appraising him with the admiration of a woman who senses herself in the presence of a virile man. This excited him, and yet each time he determined to scale the cursed moat of counters and trays, respect for her venerable mourning restrained him.

He turned from the window with a sigh. There was his desk with the scarred and stained surface, a swivel chair that perched crookedly to one side because of a broken bearing, and a pair of mismatched armchairs on the other side of the desk. On the desk was a gleaming and ornately ornamented belt of silver-buckled elegance inscribed:

FIRST PLACE,
HELLENIC WRESTLING CHAMPIONSHIP,
PITTSBURGH, PENNSYLVANIA,
May 22, 1947

There was a foot-high alabaster model of the headless and armless Aphrodite of Cyrene, whose smooth and naked buttocks even in miniature were an awesome sight. And on the corner of his desk a jar containing several handfuls of soil he had carried with him from Crete. He had kept this soil near him always, pressing it in his palm at times of anguish and receiving great strength from the fierce black earth, kneaded with the tears and blood of centuries.

The walls of the office (he had painted them himself after considerable experimental blending of colors) were an Aegean sea-green with tinges of Mediterranean purple. They were further decorated by a number of framed testimonial letters from enthusiastic clients, and some photographs of classical sculpture. His greatest pride were the paintings in dark frames of his great-grandfather and grandfather, paintings he had commissioned from a pair of old tintypes he had inherited.

The two old men were lions with flowing beards and hair that fell thickly to their shoulders and moustaches waxed into steely tips. They were cannoneered with muskets, cartridge belts, and curve-bladed yataghans. Both had been killed fighting the Turks, one in 1866 at the monastery in Arkadi, the other at Megalokastro in 1889, surrounded by the bodies of the Turkish soldiers he had slain. In a futile effort at vengeance the sultan hung his severed head on a pike outside his harem.

His family well knew the smell of powder and war. As a young girl his grandmother helped cut up the old books the monks brought from the monasteries to make cartridge cases. In 1917, a year after Matsoukas was born, his father died in Thessaly fighting the Bulgarians. In 1942 he lost his brother, Stathis, as they fought side by side in the mountains of Albania against the Italians. When the Nazis came with tanks and stukas to shore up their beaten allies, Matsoukas retreated with his companions to Crete to fight until that blessed island too succumbed. For two years afterwards he fought with the guerrillas in the mountains, making bloody forays against the German garrisons at night.

For a moment he stood before the paintings, lost in a winged recollection of those zestful days and nights. The campfires before the mountain caves, the fragrance of the lamb roasting on the spit mingled with the aroma of figs and pomegranates and the canary-yellow winter melons. The harsh husky laughter of his comrades, the cleaning of weapons before a battle, the wild joy of combat itself, the smell of powder and death gilding the earth with a keen and jubilant vigor.

Regretfully he shook off the quivering nostalgia. Twelve years ago, anxious for new experience, and determined to subdue the New World, he had emigrated to the United States. He had married, bred children, opened his business, and here he was.

He sat down at his desk carefully balancing himself in the broken chair to keep from toppling backwards. He opened the drawer and drew out a long slim dagger with a handle of glistening bone carved in the shape of a woman's bosom, two small breasts with a pair of tiny jewels imbedded as the nipples. Holding the hilt thoughtfully between his fingers, he bent finally to his mail.

Aside from the usual promotional material, there was a letter with the return address of an attorney. He slit the flap neatly with the dagger. The attorney, representing a butcher Matsoukas owed a long overdue bill, threatened immediate suit if a check in the amount of $63.00 were not received by return mail.

Matsoukas scowled at the letter and resisted an impulse to rush down to the butcher's shop a few blocks away and punch the scoundrel's fat head. Instead he brusquely drew out a sheet of his stationery with the letterhead of the PINDAR MASTER COUNSELING SERVICE and in a large showy script wrote:

Sir:

Your client is a rascal and a thief. His abominable meat nearly poisoned members of my family on three separate occasions and one time personally caused me a debilitating diarrhea for more than twenty hours.

I have long been considering a lawsuit of my own against him and your impertinent letter has made up my mind. Prepare to hear from my legal representative very soon.

He signed this with a flourish, Leonidas Matsoukas, and folded the letter into the stamped return envelope the butcher's attorney had provided.

A ripple of reflected movement in the alley made him drop the envelope. He swiveled in the chair to rise quickly, lost his balance when the broken bearing slipped, and grabbed for the corner of the desk. For half a minute he struggled furiously to keep from being flipped. He finally got his feet back on the floor, leaped up, and from the window caught a last shimmering flash of Anthoula's white shift as the door closed.

"God curse the bloody chair!" he cried and lashed out a vigorous kick that spun the seat like a revolving door and loosened several additional screws. He was so engrossed in his outrage that for a moment he did not hear the timorous knock on the door, until the knock was sounded again.

Matsoukas bent quickly to straighten the chair and sat down to bend over his mail. "Come in," he called gravely.

The old man who entered was slight of build, well-dressed in a shirt, tie, and neat brown suit. He had a pinched and dolorous face.

"Mr. Matsoukas?"

"At your service, sir," Matsoukas held firmly to the desk with both hands and rose. He extended his big fist to enfold the bony appendage of fingers the man offered.

"Telecles," the man said. "Antonio Telecles."

"Please be seated, Mr. Telecles," Matsoukas said, and motioning to one of the armchairs he walked around the desk and sat down in the other chair which he pulled around to face his visitor.

Telecles shifted in evident discomfort.

"I was told at the gambling room of Falconis that you might be able to help me," he began hesitantly. "The stud poker dealer, Cicero, spoke of you as a truly remarkable man."

Matsoukas made a gesture of seemly modesty. "A jewel of a man and my dear friend."

Telecles nodded and lapsed into silence again. Matsoukas waited discreetly.

"Mr. Matsoukas," Telecles began again and for the first time noticed the statuette of Aphrodite. He pursed his lips and blew a thin whistle of appreciation through his teeth. By concentrating on her effulgent decorations, his voice gained a measure of strength. "In the past year there has been a certain falling away of my . . ." his voice drooped sadly, ". . . power to love."

Matsoukas nodded gravely. For a moment he considered the matter thoughtfully. "How old are you, Mr. Telecles?" he asked finally.

"Seventy-one last November."

"Incredible!" Matsoukas cried. "You don't look a day over fifty. But even seventy-one for an obviously virile man like yourself should raise no question of failing powers." He raised his eyebrows. "Are you married?"

"For the third time two years ago," Telecles spoke with a generous pride in his voice.

"Bravo!" Matsoukas said. "You are living the abundant life that mighty Pindar praises in his songs."

"My present wife is just thirty-three," Telecles made an awkward fumble with his bony hand in the air to suggest a body of nubile proportions.

"Go on, my friend," Matsoukas felt himself warming to the man's plight. "Speak to me as you would confide to your physician and your priest."

Telecles leaned forward with a slight flush darkening his cheeks. "She is from Tripoli," he said. "You know the women from Tripoli are very passionate. She had a pet name for me when we first married. She used to call me . . ." he paused ruefully, ". . . Sultan."

"Normally a term of derogation," Matsoukas said sternly, "but the context in which she used it was obviously one of approbation and respect."

"Exactly!" Telecles said in fervent gratitude for Matsoukas' understanding. He wiped a vagrant tear from his eye. "Haven't heard a whisper of that name lately. Can't say I blame her either."

Matsoukas nodded in sympathy. He heard the rattle of a garbage can cover in the alley and leaped from his chair to the window in two great strides. "Getting stuffy in here!" he said loudly to Telecles as he gripped the handles of the window.

Anthoula was below in her full glory, and even as he watched she bent in graceful innocence to retrieve several scraps of paper fallen from the container. Her back was to him and her hips arched and strained against the thin white shift which spread as tight as the skin of a drum across her magnificent buttocks. Only a single fold low in the glorious crevice artfully divided one saintly twin from the other.

"Holy Zeus!" Matsoukas said fervently. Even after she had gone back into the bakery he gripped the handles of the window so rigidly that the blood left his knuckles.

"Pardon me?" Telecles said.

Matsoukas jerked the window up a few inches and turned excitedly around. "Mr. Testicles!" he cried, "I have the solution to your problem!"

"Telecles," the old man said. "Antonio Telecles."

"Right!" Matsoukas said. He closed his eyes for a moment and recalled the vision of Anthoula. "The difference between a clod and a conqueror in love," he said ardently. "Do you know, my friend, what that difference is?"

Telecles waited in a perplexed silence.

"Imagination!" Matsoukas cried. "Think of yourself as a God swept by wild desire and the woman not just a mortal drab with rubbery bubs and a patch of lank hair between her legs but a Goddess, a lovely Diana, a cyclonic Juno!" He made a valiant effort to calm himself. "But I go too quickly. The success of this Service is based on practical help, a step at a time . . . therefore it is important that you begin with a good night's sleep the evening before you decide to make love to your wife. A little nap during the following afternoon to conserve your strength and if you cannot sleep, lie awake and count the delights ahead. In the evening a light supper, a single plate of moussaka, or lamb with green beans. Then a half bottle of retsina . . . no more than that because as the great Aristotle said, 'a wet stick does not make a good fire.'"

Telecles waited in a stark and blistering suspense.

"Now you begin," Matsoukas said softly. "A few compliments first. How lovely she is. How radiant her eyes. How like a peach is her skin. A little kissing, a caressing of the ears and the eyes and the curve of the throat. A tender fondling of the marvels below. The great moment approaches."

Matsoukas extended one hand slowly with the palm up and the fingers spread. He brought his other hand to hover over it with the middle finger pointed stiffly down. Even as Telecles clutched the arms of his chair and moved his knobby knees apart, Matsoukas brought his hands together sharply, the finger of the upper hand piercing like a lance between the fingers of the hand below.

"At this moment of union," Matsoukas said fiercely, "you must lose mortal shape and become a goat with the ears, mouth, and horns of a goat. You hear the reed panpipes wailing all about you. You are a worshipper of Bacchus in a woodland of fertility and you have a ravishing nymph in your arms. Love her in that instant as if you were the God, Pan, himself!"

He bent and clutched the old man by the shoulders and brought him resonating with ardor out of his chair.

"Remember who you are!" Matsoukas cried. "You come of a race of mighty men! Look upon all of life with the

16

eye of a tiger! Let your spirit be a torch, a flame, a fiery dart! Let your loins be a golden goblet full of foaming wine!"

Telecles stood breathing in short gasps, numbed by the majestic sweep of the narrative. He nodded mutely in burning affirmation.

"That will be five dollars," Matsoukas said crisply, "and if you do not enjoy immediate improvement in your conjugal relations, my unconditional guarantee permits a second consultation absolutely free of charge."

"A second consultation will not be needed!" Telecles cried. He brought out his wallet and with trembling fingers counted out five dollar bills. He passed them to Matsoukas and then looked once more at Aphrodite, his lip curling in an ominous leer. With a handclasp of poignant farewell he took his leave.

Matsoukas looked at the five soiled bills in his hand and pulled out his own worn wallet. He inserted four of the bills in the wallet carefully, feeling a resurgence of excitement because the wretched Olympian chasm was no longer bone empty. He walked back to the desk and unlocked the upper right-hand drawer. Inside was a small metal cashbox. He added the dollar remaining from the fee to the small scatter of change and few crumpled bills within. There was a passport for Stavros and himself for Greece and a bankbook. He took out the bankbook and scanned the entry of one hundred and eleven dollars that it had taken him a year to save by putting aside twenty percent of his income. An inadequate amount beside what was needed but it was growing. A solid parlay or a hot streak at poker might put him over the top. Once in the cashbox he never touched the bills or change regardless of the urgency of his need. Twice a month he took the money to the bank and received another entry in the bankbook.

With the box locked and closed again in the drawer he thought suddenly of visiting the bakery. A press of customers might summon Anthoula from the kitchen.

He went quickly to the closet and opened the door to the small basin within. He washed his hands, whistling hoarsely, and then picked up his hairbrush. He wet the bristles under a quick spray of water and drew the brush vigorously through his thick tangled hair, groaning slightly as the strands tugged against their roots. When he finished he stared uneasily at his reflection.

His face seemed suddenly composed of a deeper darkness and shadow. It was as if the shade at the window had been partly drawn, the room about him grown darker. A strange eerie silence filled his ears. He leaned forward and tried to see into the hollows of the hidden eyes. A chill swept his flesh.

"Matsoukas, Matsoukas," he said softly. "We are things of a day. What we are and what we are not. Man is a shadow's dream."

CHAPTER TWO

MATSOUKAS descended the stairs and entered the grocery, his nostrils dilating before the pungent aroma of sharp cheeses and spiced meats. He considered purchasing a spare lunch but he wanted to retain the four dollars remaining from his fee for a wager on a choice horse. The number four had certain hortatory connotations he could not ignore.

At the same time he was hungry. He brought out what loose change he had in his pocket and counted thirty-six cents. However he tabulated the coins, the total was the same. This amount was the very least he would need to justify an excursion into the bakery.

He might exhort Akragas into releasing some cheese and lamb and a chunk of bread by promising him a share of possible winnings from the day's play. Although it had been a long time since the grocer had succumbed to such an enticement, Matsoukas knew the man's extraordinary greed made such a commitment always a possibility.

He called out the grocer's name in a tone that suggested matters of great urgency to discuss. For an instant there was no response and then Akragas came out of the cubicle in the rear of the store, tugging feebly at his shapeless pants, the sibilant rumble of water echoing behind him. It was obvious from the old man's tight and plaintive demeanor that his ritual had been a futile one. Matsoukas shrugged at the way in which fate weighted her scales and swiftly whipped a glistening ripe plum into his pocket as consolation.

"I am expecting a package from the Greek Consulate," Matsoukas said as Akragas approached. "Kindly hold it carefully for me."

"Your deportation papers?" Akragas sneered. Matsoukas waved the grocer a cheerful goodby, meanwhile stroking the plum in his pocket.

After making a bet on a broad-rumped little filly named Dolphina at one of Falconis' cigar store branches and passing over his four dollar bills, Matsoukas walked to the bakery. He stood for a moment outside the window with the reverence of a man preparing to enter church. Bracing his shoulders and rising to his full height, he took one final look at his reflection in the glass and entered the sacred portal.

He was struck as always by an awareness of how these surroundings suited Anthoula. From these warm cloisters she made sweet the bitter hungers of the world. The racks of fragrant pastries, the trays of luscious honey and nut sweets, the warm fresh marrow of dark and light breads were as much a landscape for a Goddess as any sylvan setting by a sparkling pool. Even the cupids and nymphs were there, winged tiny figures molded of sugar, quivering to spring aloft from the escarpments of frosted crocus and tulip petals that friezed the cakes.

"What's yours?" The voice was aseptic, a jarring intrusion upon his celestial reflections. Old lady Barboonis, dried by jaundice and celibacy into a yellow and withered stalk, stood across the counter from him. Matsoukas peered for a plaintive moment at the buzzer beside the register which would summon Anthoula and then turned to dazzle the old lady with a smile.

"Good morning, Mrs. Barboonis!" he said cheerfully. "You are looking your usual lovely self today."

"Save that syrup for some young tart, Matsoukas," the old lady sneered. "And I have told you fifty times it is Miss Barboonis."

"Impossible to believe!" Matsoukas stared at her incredulously. "I can never fathom how the men permitted a woman such as you to escape!"

"Strutting cocks and swaggering bulls!" The old lady spit in a cloud of scorn. "I would rather be dead than married!"

So would the poor devil who married you, Matsoukas thought. "Don't say that!" he cried. "Poor creatures as we men are we struggle all our lives to be worthy of the women we love."

"If you were to struggle a little harder when you came in here," Miss Barboonis snapped, "perhaps it would not take you half an hour to decide on one raisin cookie."

He smiled quickly to conceal the effect of the barb she had winged into his flesh. He bent and bared his teeth at a tray of splendid cakes. When the door of the bakery opened and a woman entered, he straightened up with a resurgence of hope. "Please attend to the lady," he said loudly to Miss Barboonis. He walked along the counter, whistling softly, keeping an eye on the doorway from the kitchen.

He was delighted when the front door opened again and another woman entered closely followed by two more customers. They clustered in a small group before the counter. Matsoukas felt his pulse mounting.

For a frantic moment it appeared he might be denied his pleasure. The old lady raced about on her spindly legs, counting cookies, cutting sweets, wrapping bread, breaking the string of packages with a swift snap of her hard fingers. Matsoukas was despairingly awed at the speed her withered flanks could muster.

The entrance of two additional customers, a man and a woman, decided the fray. The old lady, breathing hard, stopped directly before the buzzer, a shudder of defeat scaling her cheeks. Matsoukas, his arm partially concealed by his body, extended his finger stiffly and pressed in gleeful unison with the old lady's shove. The strident buzzing that sounded from the kitchen resonated through his body.

When Anthoula emerged from the kitchen, she was the same lovely woman he had spied upon in the alley countless times. She wore the simple white shift, her hair bound in dark lustrous braids about her head. But from the perspective of his window, her body invited lust. There was wantonness in her breasts and thighs straining against the shift and in the way her bare arms and legs glistened nakedly in the daylight.

When he came close to her he saw with a strange delight that she was chaste. Her full lips were bare of any stain, her cheeks scrubbed clean of powder and rouge, her dark eyes seemly with a virtue she had spun from the cloth of her sorrow on the loom of her loneliness. Before the shadow of her mourning, the hard thrust of his passion turned tender and he saw her body as part of a mural for the wall of heaven.

I will write you a poem, Anthoula, he thought, and pin the words like flowers in your hair.

"Good afternoon, Widow Anthoula," he spoke gravely without a trace of a smile. She replied with no more than a courteous nod but a faint flush glittered for a moment in her cheeks. She spoke to one of the customers and bent to raise a platter of baklava to the counter.

"Make up your mind yet, Matsoukas?" Miss Barboonis was back, sour and stringy, eyes like dried and wrinkled prunes.

"Give me a kouloura," he said, with his eyes still unwilling to abandon Anthoula. "There is nobody in this city," he said loudly, "who bakes a better kouloura than Widow Anthoula."

This time there was no mistaking the warmth that curled into her cheeks. He felt a fever of weakness sweep his legs.

Miss Barboonis handed him the wrapped kouloura. "Fifty-two cents," she said.

A groan threatened to burst from his throat when he remembered the thirty-six cents in his pocket. By an incredible feat of histrionics he converted the groan to a twisted smile.

"On second thought, dear lady," he said smoothly, "perhaps I better not take the entire kouloura. It is more than I can eat and will become stale."

"Is this some kind of game?" the old lady snarled.

"You've been here a half-hour now. You finally make up your mind . . ."

Anthoula came to the old lady and touched her arm. "If a full loaf is too much for Mr. Matsoukas," she said, "we will be pleased to sell him half a loaf." She looked at him and he saw the glistening splendor of her eyes.

"You are very kind," Matsoukas said. With his flesh trembling he considered how it would feel to unbraid her hair and let it tumble free about her shoulders.

The old lady tore off the paper about the bread and picked up a long bladed knife. With a look at Matsoukas suggesting there were other things she might prefer to sever, she balefully cut the loaf in half.

"I must pay the full price anyway," Matsoukas said to Anthoula. "The entire fifty-two cents."

Anthoula shook her head.

"I insist!" Matsoukas cried scorning caution and restraint. "Let me pay for all and give the half to some needy child."

"Let him pay," the old lady slapped the wrapped half-loaf on the counter. "Help him make up his mind next time."

"Half a loaf is half the price of a whole loaf," Anthoula said firmly. She took the change from his hand and the soft tips of her fingers grazed his palm. Even that fleeting touch reverberated through the length of his body and a quiver swept her breasts as well. She turned away quickly and rang up the twenty-six cents on the small register. Without looking at him again she started back to the kitchen. He watched her marvelous buttocks swaying with a winged and rolling grace. He sighed and found the

24

old lady watching him with a hard awareness in her dried prune eyes.

"Many thanks, Miss Barboonis," he said. "I will enjoy this bread."

The old lady grinned a toothless and unspoken leer that drove him in a disruptive retreat from the bakery, clutching the segment of kouloura against his heart.

He sat on a corner bench across from a schoolyard at noon and ate the half-loaf of kouloura. He tore the bread into chunks that he washed down with coffee he had purchased with his sole remaining dime. For dessert he ate the plum slowly and watched the children at their lunch-hour play.

The yard teemed with boys and girls of varied ages and assorted sizes. Yet all had in common an incredible agility, a marvelous nimbleness, their arms and legs flashing as they swarmed and scattered and screamed and ran. They skimmed and swooped like myriad butterflies above the earth, and he thought of his son, Stavros, a small black moth pinned to the ground in a raging shell.

He recalled the beginning, the sunburst moment when the child was born. The wild delight of those first months fondling the baby, playing with him, watching him grow. Until the dreadful nights when the child began clawing frantically at his eyes, pulling furiously at his ears. Each month revealing more of the savage impediments that stifled speech and made him flounder like a small crippled crab. The strange laughter without a smile, the eruption of weird sound from between the prison of his lips.

Hope scalded and withered with each visit to the doctors until Matsoukas ceased listening and treated the boy with his own will and spirit. The hours he spent talking to him, singing to him, dancing with him to crack the shell of total withdrawal that threatened to engulf him. The labor of a year of such hours to achieve the clumsy knocking together of two boxes. Another year so the boy might hit a suspended bell. Two more years before he could pound into a block, a single large peg, achieve a few added movements of the arms, a few additional graspings with his fingers. So much more than the cursed doctors had ever expected could be accomplished but so little measured by what needed to be done. Yet he had never lost faith. Long after even Caliope had tearfully abandoned hope, he had never lost faith that his son would someday gain movement and speech.

For he knew the roots were strong, the ground was fertile, his seed was part of the olive, the myrtle, the honeycomb, and the huge luscious grapes. His heart contained the wind and the stars. The stream of his blood ran through the enchanted caves where nymphs played, over jagged promontories on which wild shepherds danced, into valleys stained with the blood of heroes and giants.

The screams of the children grew wilder and he could not endure watching them any longer. He rose and for a moment looked in anguish at the gray heavy sky. He cried out a fierce oath and then walked quickly down the street, his head bent, until the voices of the children were lost within the horns and rumble of the city. When he could hear them no longer he straightened up and briskly paced the blocks to the Minoan Music Shop.

He entered the door beneath the dust-crusted sign that swayed in creaking rondos to the wind. The interior was a maze of racks and alcoves, shadowed shelves laden with sheafs of sheet music undisturbed for years. The walls held faded concert posters of Caruso and Galli-Curci. From a hidden corner a shrill phonograph scratched out a tuneless song.

Matsoukas moved deftly down the aisles, around the corners, between the shelves, to the alcove where the owner, Falconis, sat at a paper-littered desk.

"I beg your pardon," Matsoukas said. "Do you have a recording of, 'Forty Years a Married Virgin,' by that world-famous soprano, Ena Meros Adeio?"

Falconis sighed. He was a somber-visaged man with the eyes of a sparrow in a landscape of hawks.

"I have no time for your sad jokes, Matsoukas."

"That is the trouble with you," Matsoukas said. "Laughter is therapeutic. Man reaches fulfillment, society gains balance, children learn to sing, all through laughter. It is a catharsis and a means of purifying the bile of the spirit."

"You wish to play or to lecture?"

"I did not come here to purchase one of your cracked records," Matsoukas shrugged.

Falconis motioned toward the bottom drawer of his desk which contained the ledger of his accounts. "There is the matter of your debt," Falconis said coldly. "You know the house rules."

"The curse of modern life," Matsoukas said. "A mother-in-law, the devil, and debts." He made a casual movement with his hand as if reaching for the pocket which contained his wallet. "By the way, old sport, I think you understand that when honor is concerned, I always pay in the end."

"You will pay soon or be faced with a dreadful beating," Falconis sought to mask his timid eyes with a glint of menace.

Matsoukas laughed loudly and reached across the desk. Falconis flinched in fear and then relaxed sheepishly as Matsoukas clapped him gently on the shoulder.

"You are not suited by temperament for violence," Matsoukas said.

Falconis looked mournfully at the soft cushions of fat nestled across his palms. "How wretchedly true," he said softly. "If I had been born a few hundred miles west of Greece I might have sprung roots in Roman soil. My name might as easily have been Falconelli and I might have become one of those stalwarts chosen for that illustrious organization, the Mafia." A wistful longing swept his face. "The Greeks are incapable of such unity and dedication."

"Do not despair," Matsoukas said soothingly. "Join the Board of Trustees of some of the Hellenic churches. They include men eagerly emulating your idols." He looked impatiently at the drapes which concealed the panel leading to the other rooms. "By the way, old sport," he said. "How much is my tab?"

"You know very well," Falconis said. "Four-hundred and eighty-three dollars." He coughed as if mention of the amount caused him an obstructive disorder in his throat. "I cannot understand how I let it go so far."

"Very soon now I will clear it off your books," Matsoukas said. "In fact I feel fate tingling a bountiful bell before me today. I have a solid bet going on a marvelous little filly but if she has lost, perhaps a small additional advance to . . ."

"Not another dime!" Falconis exclaimed.

"How can I repay you if I do not play?"

"That is what you told me four hundred dollars ago," Falconis said. "Look where we are now. This kind of credit can ruin my reputation." He fell silent and when he spoke again a note of apology had entered his voice. "Don't count too much on my not having a temperament for violence. That is what I pay Youssouf for."

"That Turkish gorilla has been hungering to eat my kidneys for years," Matsoukas said. "One of these days we will determine who eats what."

"Don't underestimate him because he is a clown," Falconis said darkly. "He has the strength of three bulls. I have seen men he has beaten in that dreadful basement below us. They are not men anymore."

"Get rid of the animal," Matsoukas said. "If you need muscle hire a good Greek gorilla."

"Do you think I like the beast around?" Falconis looked uneasily over his shoulder at the panel. "He chills my blood but he also chills the blood of others. What can I do? I am a mouse and the cats would gobble me if I did not keep a wild dog." He shook his head dolefully and bent to press a button beneath the center drawer of his desk. The panel behind him slipped smoothly aside and Matsoukas walked into a high-ceilinged and cavernous room. The panel closed swiftly and silently behind him. He felt as he always did when he first stepped through the opening that he had entered the teeming landscape of another world and the lunge of his spirit broke loose with a wild cry.

It was Nepheloccygia, the city of birds, the "Cloud-cuckoo-borough," of Aristophanes. All were gathered in this room, the owl, jay, lark, thyme-finch, ring-dove,

29

chicken and cuckoo, the feathered company of dark-winged dreamers, pigeons of the scratch sheet tip and sparrows of the fifty-cents-across-the-board-parlay. Around them lurked the falcons and hawks, the ticket writers and spotters perched on high stools behind the long counter, their heads poised sharply as beaks.

The birds milled about until the Lydian flute of the wire service announcer erupted over the loudspeaker with the running of a race. Then they scattered to flight, swarming before the wall on which the track sheet was tacked. They waited and beat their wings in frenzy at the calls and now and then uttered shrill wild cries.

Matsoukas swept through them, joining the fever of their bodies to his own flesh, answering their greetings with a flutter of his shoulders, a smile, a nod.

"Anything good today, Matsoukas?" An old woman with fingers like talons caught at his shoulder.

"If we are lucky, mother, a glass of wine for supper," Matsoukas said.

"Can Salmi beat Maud Princess on a muddy track?" A young man called to him.

"Only at a mile or more," Matsoukas said. "And no more weight than a hundred-twenty."

"Want something hot in the third?" A tout who did not know him whispered.

"Away from me, buzzard!" Matsoukas cried. The man scurried away with his feathers ruffled. A few of the men and women around them laughed.

Matsoukas moved beyond the clutching hands and the restless eyes and walked to the chart that listed the day's races at Monmouth. His heart gave a small gratified leap when he saw that his little filly, Dolphina, had won. He walked jubilantly to the end of the room where the pale bespectacled cashier sat behind his ledger and the cash-drawer. On a stool at his side sat the Turk, Youssouf.

He was built like a massive wild boar, huge-boned with immense ridges of muscle the length of his powerful body. He had a totally bald head, glistening with a coating of some green heavy oil. The waxed tips of a long moustache hung suspended over the tusks of his teeth.

When he saw Matsoukas he grinned and the corners of his wide mouth cut almost to the twisted lobes of his shapeless wrestler's ears, giving him the droll appearance of a clown. But the fool's mask could not conceal his eyes, small and deep and almost without pupils, their gaze sharpened by cold and transparent lids.

"Hey, Matsoukas," he said, and his voice came in a mirthless banter from his throat. "How's the old whoreson Greek?"

"Who is your bubbling companion?" Matsoukas asked the cashier. "He has all the charm of a squid."

The cashier looked nervously at Youssouf and fumbled through his book. "Matsoukas," he read the entry. "Four to win on Dolphina. She paid $23.80 for two. You got $47.60 coming."

"You are a wizard!" Matsoukas said. "Keep up the good work and someday you may become bookkeeper in a Turkish whorehouse."

Youssouf leaned forward and winked with a frozen lidding of one eye. "I got a little Greek dancer girlfriend, Matsoukas," he said. "I screw her six maybe seven times a night. She won't even spit on a Greek anymore."

Matsoukas smiled and turned back to the cashier who

was counting out the money quickly with his Adam's apple bobbing.

"Any talent in the back room?" Matsoukas asked him.

"The usual bunch," the cashier said. "And a new fellow I never seen before. They call him the 'Fig King'."

"We must not keep a 'Fig King' waiting," Matsoukas said. He pocketed the bills and started away, pausing thoughtfully before the Turk.

"I tell you something, gorilla," Matsoukas said pleasantly. "You stink like a maggot's picnic. You know? I tell you as a friend that a bath in batshit would improve you."

The cashier slid off his stool in a frenzy to get out of the way. The clown's mask left Youssouf's face, a scabbed savage hate taking its place. He clenched his massive fists until the knuckles gleamed like white stones.

"Greek," he said, and a few drops of spittle foamed in the corners of his mouth. "Someday, Greek, I am going to kill you."

Matsoukas felt the hair along his arms and back bristle with rage. At the same time a strange tight quiver of fear swept his body.

"Turk," he said slowly and spit the word through his teeth. "Someday, Turk, you will try."

CHAPTER THREE

For a moment Matsoukas absorbed the suspensive beauty of the warm and cloistered room, a windowless nest secure from the world. In the center of the room a large round table of walnut, the green felt surface lit under the beam from a drop cord light in the ceiling with a fan shade around the bulb.

There was the soft echo of the dealer's litany calling the fall of the cards, the trails of smoke rising in silver coils to merge into a swirling cloud above the light, the smell of tobacco and sweat. And on the green felt surface of the table the frivolous one-eyed jacks flirting with the elusive queens under the eyes of the somber kings. Around the edges of the cards the fingers of the players glittered, their hands severed at the wrist by the perimeter of darkness just outside the circle of light.

Matsoukas knew the hands without seeing the faces of the men. There were the plump and clumsy fingers of Fatsas who could not win for losing, the dark leathery fingers of the guitarist, Charilaos, curling as if he were striking chords, the desultory fingers of Poulos who played

33

to pass the time and the never-resting fingers of Babalaros who played to keep from going mad. A pair of soft and diamond-studded hands, strange to him but with a certain pomposity, he apportioned to the "Fig King." And, finally, the hands of the dealer, his dear friend, Cicero, a small and frail-bodied man with a thin pale fleshed face but with slender and beautiful fingers, long and supple, the flesh gleaming like marble in moonlight, holding the deck as a king might hold his scepter, with a grave and leisured grace.

As Matsoukas passed around the table, the "Fig King" raked in a pot and smiled genially.

"My apologies, gentlemen," he said. "Since I play for sport and not to win, I do this to you reluctantly."

Cicero smiled wryly and gathered the cards for the deal.

Matsoukas sat down in a chair against the wall beside a chair in which old Gero Kampana dozed with his scarred and ancient head tilted slightly to the side. The old man had been abstemious in all facets of his life but cards, playing poker for seventy-five of his ninety years. He had never married, never given any woman more than embers from the fire of his true love. Now grown blind and deaf he could no longer distinguish the faces of the cards or hear the dealer's call. Still he sat most of the day and night in the room where cards were played, assimilating in some disordered way the rhythms and the tensions. As Matsoukas sat down he raised his head with a start.

"Who is that?" he asked peering toward the light.

"Matsoukas."

"I knew it was you," the old man snapped.

"Of course," Matsoukas said and patted the old man's knee.

For almost forty minutes he sat and watched the game and studied the play of the "Fig King." He watched him through a score of stud poker hands, fifteen of which he won. When Babalaros was driven from the game, Matsoukas rose and took his place.

He winked fondly at Cicero, nodded and greeted Charilaos and Poulos, and slapped Fatsas on the shoulder. "How are you, old sport?" He asked cheerfully. "Still playing your canny and skillful game?"

"I'm still losing if that's what you mean," Fatsas said with irritation.

Matsoukas smiled benignly at the "Fig King." "Play for sport," he said politely. "Those were your words, sir, and I completely agree." He rose slightly in his chair and bowed. "I am Leonidas Matsoukas."

"Poker for sport!" Fatsas said incredulously.

The "Fig King" extended his hand limply to Matsoukas who shook it vigorously. "Elias Roumbakakis," the tycoon said gravely. "One must be able to afford to lose," he said. "Only then is the game a sport. Do you agree?"

"Absolutely!" Matsoukas said. He peered closely at Roumbakakis. "Your face is very familiar," he said. "Tell me, sir, were you not in last Sunday's National Herald?"

"Not this last Sunday," Roumbakakis said, "although they often have my photo with dignitaries. Perhaps you saw my recent photo in the Ahepa Magazine? I was presenting a basket of figs to Alderman Pasofski, a very close friend."

Cicero bent his head and smiled crookedly as he raked in the cards.

"That must be where I saw you!" Matsoukas said. He stared somberly around the table at the other players. "I hope you all appreciate what a singular honor it is," he said, "to be playing with such an eminent leader of the Hellenic community."

Roumbakakis raised his hand in a silent demurrer but could not conceal the pleased flush that sprouted in his cheeks.

"Get a new deck and let's play!" Fatsas said to Cicero. "I'm ninety dollars out. Let's get on with this bloody sport!"

Cicero ripped the cellophane wrapping from a new deck of Bicycles and threw the jokers out. Matsoukas watched with pleasure the way his long pale fingers shuffled in a dancing rhythm, the cards becoming an extension of his hands, slicing between one another in swift sure passage.

Old Gero Kampana raised his head and sniffed the air. "New deal!" he cried with delight. "New deal!"

Cicero passed the deck to Fatsas for the cut. Then he rapped the table lightly to signal the deal. He held the deck securely in his hand and with a deft snapping motion of his fingers skimmed the cards toward the players, each card coming to rest face down before each man's money. At the end of the round he barely altered the position of his fingers and the second card was pitched face up with the corner just touching the rim of the first card.

"Queen, ten, five, eight, jack," Cicero quietly called the quick and silent fall of the cards. "Queen bets."

With a five as the highest of his first two cards, Matsoukas folded.

"You play cautiously," Roumbakakis chided him.

"We are doomed to the dictates of our natures," Matsoukas smiled. "Mine is cautious, conservative."

Fatsas released a snort. When Roumbakakis looked sharply at him, he stared innocently at his cards.

"The game loses savor when played cautiously," Roumbakakis said. "I like to play by driving forward boldly. That is the Greek tradition in warfare and in life." He won the pot by pairing his queen on the last card. Fatsas threw in his jacks with disgust. Charilaos sighed. Poulos stared idly at his fingernails.

Fatsas threw in a dollar ante somberly. "Forty years I have been married to these pasteboard bastards and bitches," he said. "Nothing but grief and despair."

"A man makes his own destiny," Roumbakakis smiled broadly showing an awesome structure of gold fillings.

If I could pluck a few of those, Matsoukas thought, they would carry Stavros and me three times to Greece. "The gold of Troy," he said aloud.

"Pardon me?" Roumbakakis said, fearing there was a compliment he might have missed.

"This game is becoming a bloody bridge session," Fatsas grumbled. "A man can't concentrate on the bloody cards."

"Your disposition is less than congenial," Roumbakakis snapped. "The way in which a man loses reveals his character."

"Jack-five, ten-nine possible straight, pair of sixes, king-seven possible flush," Cicero called. "Pair of sixes bet."

37

Matsoukas played no-stay for the next seven hands. He could not afford to remain without a solid pair. One hand he held to the fifth card feeling certain that Roumbakakis was preparing nervously to bluff. He bet lightly into the "Fig King."

"Your five and twenty dollars more," Roumbakakis said.

Matsoukas hesitated, to suggest indecision and then, as if agitated by his prudent nature, turned his cards over.

Roumbakakis laughed with delight and scooped in the pot. His flushed cheeks were clear evidence he had pulled off a bluff.

They played through the afternoon. Big Carl, heavy-bodied and lynx-eyed, replaced Cicero for an hour. When Cicero returned he walked a little unsteadily toward the table and a certain limpness marked his lips. Matsoukas looked at him with concern but his fingers did not waver as he resumed the deal. In his absence Matsoukas had strengthened his stake by winning about a hundred and fifty dollars.

The tide turned against Roumbakakis and he began to lose. He continued to play as boldly as he had played when he had been winning and lost quickly and heavily. Matsoukas began to win more steadily and little by little the hands narrowed into a battle between the "Fig King" and himself. Fatsas and Charilaos and Poulos dropped from the game and the two of them played on alone with the limit raised to fifty dollars. Falconis had entered the room and stood watching silently, a slight nervous twitch in his cheeks.

"Your twenty and raise you thirty," Matsoukas said.

Roumbakakis cursed under his breath and put in thirty dollars. With a sharp look at Matsoukas he threw in three more tens. "Back to you," he said.

"Triple ten raise to the sevens," Cicero said quietly.

"Of course," Matsoukas smiled. "Add fifty more to that." He put eighty dollars into the pot.

Roumbakakis trembled with agitation and frustration. He cleared his throat with the sound of ice being crunched. He threw in the fifty dollars almost in defiance and flipped over his cards.

"Aces and fours," he said.

"Three sevens," Matsoukas said gravely.

"Three of a kind again!" Roumbakakis cried and slammed the table with his fist. The cards and money jumped.

"New deal!" Gero Kampana came awake with a cry. "New deal!"

Roumbakakis signaled impatiently for the game to resume. All his amiability had fled and he played with a harsh and reckless anger. The next hand he bet senselessly against a pair of jacks and lost seventy dollars to Matsoukas by remaining after he knew he was beaten. When his fury had robbed him of any capacity to play effectively he rose violently from his chair which fell backwards and struck the floor. Falconis scurried to retrieve it.

"I cannot play for peanuts!" Roumbakakis said hoarsely. "I wish to play no-limit! I will put all my resources in this game and we will see!"

Falconis approached the table and Cicero looked at Matsoukas.

"No," Matsoukas said quietly. "We will allow the fifty dollar limit to remain or we will stop."

"You are afraid!" Roumbakakis cried.

"Man, you are unbalanced by anger," Matsoukas said patiently. "You could lose a small fortune before you regained your rattled senses. It would be plucking feathers from a dead pigeon."

"Who are you to tell me what I am?" Roumbakakis shouted. "I am a man of considerable prominence in this city. I have intimate friends in City Hall. I demand to play no-limit!"

"Not with me," Matsoukas said and calmly began to count the sheaf of bills before him. Roumbakakis watched quivering with fury.

"Perhaps tomorrow," Falconis said shrilly. "The house will be honored to host the game again tomorrow."

"Six hundred-forty," Matsoukas said. "Six hundred-fifty and the final twenty makes a total of six hundred-seventy dollars." He smiled amiably at Roumbakakis. "The way in which a man loses reveals his character," he said. "I am pleased you take it with such grace."

Falconis cleared his throat nervously. Cicero glared at the "Fig King" with contempt.

Matsoukas turned and handed the major sheaf of bills to Falconis. "We are square, old sport," he said and sadly he watched the money that could have taken Stavros and himself to Greece disappear quickly into Falconis' pocket. Matsoukas put away the balance of the money consoled by the hundred and twenty dollars that would go into his travel box. He started for the door with a final grin at Roumbakakis.

"I see it all now," Roumbakakis said hoarsely. "I realize that I have been involved in a game with . . . with a cheat!"

Cicero let loose a fierce tight cry. His pale face was livid with fury, his lips as sharp as the blade of a knife. He lunged at the "Fig King" with his thin arms flailing the air. Matsoukas moved swiftly and caught him in the cradle of his arm. He held him gently but firmly as the dealer struggled to break free.

"Let me at him!" Cicero cried. "I will tear off his goddam jackass ears!"

"All right now," Matsoukas sought to console him. "It's all right, my friend. The bloody twit isn't worth a blow." Still restraining Cicero he turned to Roumbakakis. "Listen to me, 'Fig King'," he said softly, "when you make an allegation against me you also slander a dealer who is known all over the country for the relentless honesty of his deal. For that reason I will enlighten your ignorance." He paused. "While you have been accumulating figs I have spent some considerable time playing bank craps, open craps, blackjack, roulette, chemin de fer, baccarat, gin rummy, poker, draw and stud, keno and the match game. I have bet on horse races, lotteries, sweepstakes, pools, raffles, and varied and assorted carnival and amusement park games."

Roumbakakis shrugged scornfully as if the information confirmed his own observation.

"Take the game in question, stud poker," Matsoukas said. "To suggest that I am a card carpenter, that I have thimble-rigged, switched, palmed, or stacked any card in the play is a stupid impertinence. To suggest that you have been trimmed, fleeced, flushed, and clipped requires an incredible pomposity. To cheat in a game with you is to resort to an enema for a sliver in my finger."

Roumbakakis flushed and opened his mouth to cry out. Matsoukas cut him off sharply.

"You are not listening," Matsoukas said. "Poker is a skill, and your arrogance, incompetence, and pomposity doom you to what you are in this game and will always be ... a bird, a greenie, a rabbit, and a pigeon."

"Hold on now!" Roumbakakis cried in an outraged voice.

"Let me clip the bastard just once!" Cicero pleaded for Matsoukas to release him.

"Hold him, Matsoukas," Falconis pleaded.

"I will spell it out in figs," Matsoukas said to Roumbakakis. "Poker is a game of deception, strategy, mathematics, and psychology. You play it as a game of chance, alibis, frets, frowns, and squawks."

Roumbakakis tried to form words to answer but no sound passed his lips. His face had grown darker, his eyes strangely glazed, and he chewed helplessly against the fillings of his gold teeth.

Matsoukas prodded Cicero—who had quieted slightly—toward the door. He turned in a final summary to Roumbakakis. "My advice to you, old sport," he said, "is to avoid poker. Find another game at which you might hope to achieve some modest success. Marbles with cross-eyed donkeys and demand they pass a saliva test at the end of each round lest your grievances accumulate and cause you to fart away the gas of your bloody figs."

For a long moment after he finished the room remained totally still. Roumbakakis released his breath in fitful spurts. Fatsas and Charilaos and Poulos tried to suppress their grins. Matsoukas let the dealer go with a final look of warning. Cicero cast a scornful glare at the "Fig King" and started for the door. Matsoukas followed him, and Falconis moved quickly out of their way.

"New deal!" Gero Kampana cried. "New deal!" And the old man's voice rose and became a wail that echoed and reechoed in the dark corners of the room.

CHAPTER FOUR

NIGHT fallen solidly across the city. The midway hour between six and midnight darkening the mouths of alleys, shrouding doorways, and enveloping the girders of the elevated. The store windows dark, people passing reflected dimly in the glass. Beams of light sweeping from cars across the litter in the gutters.

Through the evening Matsoukas came with long strong strides, hoarsely singing a martial song, ignoring the rebuking or amused glances of men and women whose paths he crossed. His arms, spread wide, were laden with large brown paper bags and money clashed metal in his pockets, no nickels, dimes, quarters or half-dollars but the deep resounding jangle of silver dollars. He whipped around the corner, his voice hurling from between the bags, freezing a heavy woman in a feathered crow's nest who lurched aside to keep from being run down. She stopped to glare after him with her battlemented head quivering in outrage.

"Drunken pig!" she shouted.

"Forgive me, my lovely!" Matsoukas called and then skipped adroitly to dodge another man. He paused an instant before the cigar store, breathing deeply the bracing ferments of aromatic tobacco. He considered stopping for a tin of imported Schimmelpennincks and then decided to hurry on. He entered the doorway beside the cigar store entrance, shifting the bags slightly to grip them more firmly as he started up the four flights of stairs. He took the steps two at a time, bags bouncing in his arms as he hummed in rhythm to the jumps. Before his door he set one bag down, brought out his key and inserted it in the lock, swinging the door open wide.

"I am here!" he cried. He picked up the bag and entered the kitchen as if he were an actor sweeping onto a stage for the opening scene of a great play. He kicked the door closed behind him.

The kitchen was full of steam, the aroma of mustard greens pungent in the air. His wife, Caliope, had her back to him and was washing a basin of soiled dishes. The dark drab housedress she wore hung limply at her knees and wrinkled across her broad and girdled hips.

"I am here!" Matsoukas repeated. He put the bags down on the table with a loud thump.

Caliope responded with a weary shrug of her shoulders. Matsoukas walked to her and stroked her bottom lightly. She looked at him then with cold black eyes.

"Forgive me," he said with a leer. "I come laden with provisions to fill our larder and feel I have certain rights."

"I know all about your rights," she said, and turned to face him fully for the first time, pushing aside a long strand of dark hair fallen loose across her cheek.

"This kitchen smells of turpentine," he said. "Did your mother brew some of her heinous herbs for the children's supper again? That stuff would turn a dragon green."

45

Instead of answering she rustled a corner of one of the bags he had carried in.

"Just a few groceries," he said.

Still watching him she reached into the bag and brought out a smaller bag of peaches and a block of white feta cheese. She stared down at what remained in the bag and then raised her head in a snap of impatience. "Wine and cheese and fruit," she said scornfully. "Children do not live on wine and cheese and fruit."

"My father's children did," Matsoukas snorted. "Grew up strong as bulls on that menu. Your loony mother raised you differently."

"The children need meat and milk," Caliope said, and he saw the surfaces of her eyes, the black pupils he always found hazardous to try and stare down. "What will I buy meat and milk with tomorrow?"

He looked at her for a long measured moment as if sadly scourging her lack of faith. He reached into his pocket and brought out a silver dollar. He placed it on the corner of the table with a loud metallic ring.

"One," he said gravely. He reached into his pocket and brought out another dollar. "Two," he said. He kept excavating with solemn ritual until there were thirty-six silver dollars lined up in a glittering rank. Fumbling in his pocket to determine the number left, he hesitated, torn between retaining a small stake for the following day's races or making his infrequent triumph as majestic an event as he could. He succumbed to the unrelenting hardness of Caliope's eyes and counted out his last six dollars to make a total of forty-two.

"I need the rest," he said, tapping lightly at his empty pocket to suggest it contained more.

She reached forward and with a peremptory sweep of her strong bare arm drove the dollars into the pocket of her frock where they hung like the swollen udder of a cow. He stared at them with a poignant sense of loss. He stepped in to kiss her, and she turned her head so he would not have her mouth. A scent of oil and sweat rose from her pores and a desire for her ridged his flesh.

"Perhaps you are wondering about the money," he said, "and why I could not be here for supper. Well, I had a splendid day. Clients kept me busy all afternoon, and through the evening, most of them eager to return for future appointments. A brilliant young student wished assistance in translating some of Pindar's poetry and the Greek Consul sent the youth to me."

"If he actually did recommend you," the searing voice of his mother-in-law erupted behind him, "they should recall the bloody fool and shoot him as he gets off the boat."

"Good evening, Mama!" Matsoukas cried with a travesty of a courtly bow. "All day I am tormented by the thought that something might permanently close your blessed and saintly mouth!"

The old lady answered with a snarl. She was in her middle sixties, sturdier than many women half her age. She had eyes like powder horns and a mouth curved like a scimitar. (Matsoukas swore she was festooned with a disposition to give a man scurvy.) Since she felt nakedness more indecent than murder, she wore black dresses high around her throat and low about her ankles. She scorned all recreation except the death notices, which she read with silent intensity until the sight of a familiar name made her quiver with the ardor of a bride.

47

Matsoukas ignored her and spoke to Caliope. "There were a number of clients who paid me in cash."

"Clients, is it!" the old lady spit. "Who would bring you anything besides a barren sow?" She snorted, the closest sound to laughter she had achieved in forty years. "I warned you," she said balefully to Caliope. "You wouldn't listen. You followed him like a heifer in heat. Look at you now. God help your children if I didn't have a few dollars from my blessed husband's insurance to provide this house."

"Blessed husband?" Matsoukas snickered. "The poor devil died in desperation to escape!" He gave her a rampant grin. "Thirty years of your groundhog teats and porcupine hump must make him feel that Hell is Miami Beach."

The old lady opened her mouth and released a savage cacophony of outrage and curses.

Caliope turned wearily to the sink again to scrub the dishes with a worn cloth, her fingers submerging slowly into the suds.

"Listen to the old crow croak," Matsoukas said amiably when the old lady ran out of breath, "I think it loosens her bowels."

Their voices had risen and his daughters, Faith and Hope, came shrieking to greet him. One clutched his leg and the other jumped to reach the bags on the table.

"Get down!" he laughed with a playful tug at Hope's curls. "Let go, you little crocodile!"

As they kept up their shrill cries, Caliope turned from the sink. "Stop it!" she shouted. "Do you hear me?" She reached down and with her hand dripping suds gave Faith a stinging smack across her bottom. Faith howled in shock and retreated to join her sister in hugging their father's legs.

"Mama's right," Matsoukas said. "Now quiet down." He gave them both a broad wink and stroked the tip of his moustache. "If you both finished all your supper I have brought you a surprise for dessert. Ice cream for good little darlings."

Faith started to shriek again but a warning look from Caliope made her close her mouth. She joined her sister in pulling with silent frenzy at the bag.

Matsoukas started past the old lady in the doorway who stared venomously at him. Her mouth opened and a final low and sibilant curse spit at him. He reached out slyly as if he were going to sneak a pinch at the nipple of her mailed breast. She grunted and swung her arms like war clubs to defend her imperiled bosom. Matsoukas roared with laughter and walked briskly down the long shadowed hall.

He passed the bedroom where Faith and Hope had been playing in a litter of half-dressed dolls. From the floor he picked up a pair of paint-chipped toy telephones. He carried them to the arched entrance of the parlor.

His son, Stavros, was awkwardly slouched in a corner of the high-barred bed, his back to his father, his face inclined toward the dark square of the high center window. One small slim-boned foot was clad in a cotton stocking, the other foot was bare, a glistening whiteness to the toes. His neck was thin and frail, and a strip of pale flesh separated the dark curly nape of his hair from the brown cotton of his shirt. One hand was hinged upon the other, a crayon dangling from the crevice formed by his palm and fingers.

49

Matsoukas went to stretch his arms over the bars, gathered the boy gently into the nest of his hands, and kissed his hair and throat. Stavros stirred and moved his head in tight small jerks. Matsoukas felt the child's tremor of recognition sweep his own flesh.

He was handsome, soft-haired, with a fine small nose and tiny shapely ears and cherubic lips. But the watery eyes, the strangely limned eyes, the pupils like black buttons in a broken shell, gave his face a wound of dullness.

His elbows fluttered from his side. His hands flailed the air pulling his body forward. His fingers, bent in the shape of a claw, caught the pad of paper fallen against the bars and dragged it closer before losing it. A thin shrill wail split his lips.

"I can see what you have been doing!" Matsoukas cried and raised the pad to stare jubilantly at the chaotic scrawls. "Good! Good!" He kissed the boy again and fondled his hair.

He put one of the toy telephones into the bed at the boy's ankles. He held the other phone and knelt, resting his cheek against the bars. He put the phone to his ear and mouth and waited.

Stavros stared at him for a moment and then tore his gaze toward the phone. He looked at it for a long time and then fluttered his fingers over his knees toward it. He caught it once and lost it.

"Good! Good!" Matsoukas nodded furiously.

Stavros managed to brace the phone between his knees. He swayed awkwardly forward, bending almost double, until his mouth came close to the receiver. His lips quivered and sucked for air.

"Hello! Hello!" Matsoukas spoke loudly into his phone. "This is Mr. Poupouloupis! Who am I talking to? Who am I talking to if you please?"

The boy's mouth opened, his teeth glittered, and breath came in a tuneless hissing from between his tensed lips.

"Mr. Stavros!" Matsoukas cried. "Just the gentleman I wanted to talk to. I have good news for you, Mr. Stavros. One hundred twenty-three more dollars goes into our bank!" He whistled in exultation. "One hundred twenty-three more dollars for our flight! Do you hear, Mr. Stavros?"

The boy strained again toward the phone, his body bent tight as a bow, a vein wriggling like a small dark worm in the paleness of his temple.

"We will celebrate, my son!" Matsoukas cried softly. "Mr. Poupouloupis has brought you ice cream!" He grinned in rampant pleasure and rubbed his stomach with a moan of joy.

He saw the boy strangely alert in that moment, the wistfulness of a huge delight trembling just beneath his flesh. Stavros moved then, falling to the side, his hands clawing between the bars of the bed, his fingers plunging toward his father.

With a soft torn cry Matsoukas rose and swept the boy from the bed. He held him tightly while the boy's fingers groped over the fabric of the suit, caressing the wool, seeking to curl beneath the cloth.

"Ice cream!" Matsoukas said. "Ice cream!" He began to rock the boy back and forth in rhythm to the words. "Ice cream! Ice cream!"

The shades flapped suddenly at the windows and he felt the beat of his own pulse. Shadows pressed around

51

the frames and he heard the wild and demonic cry of the wind. The light began to fail and the blackness sprang to close around them.

"Ice cream!" he cried. "Ice cream for my son!" He held the boy bound in his arms and began to dance, his feet shuffling and gliding in a strange and dismembered movement. In the corner the lamplight wavered and the room hung suspended between shades of darkness and light.

He danced around the rim of darkness, between the whipping tails of shadow, and in the glass of the windows grotesque reflections twirled and mimicked his steps. He danced on, the rhythm growing wilder, the walls and the floors shifting with his whirling, the light growing brighter, moonless midnight receding. Then he was free, broken away into the arch of the sky, dancing beyond the myriads of fixed stars, ascending toward the core of a blazing sun.

And in his arms, riding the crest of the flight, Stavros fluttered his frail shoulders and like a new-winged bird strained to burst his fetters and spring aloft.

Later that night with the children sleeping and the asthmatic snores of the old lady rumbling through the flat, Matsoukas followed Caliope into their bedroom and closed and locked the door.

He stripped off his clothes and stood completely naked. He flexed his muscles, looking down at the hard washboard of his belly. Satisfied there was no trace of fat yet apparent, he swung his hands to the floor and kicked his feet to the ceiling. He hung there, swaying slightly, the hair along his chest and legs gaining a sudden sharpened vigor.

"I see you, bull-balls!" Matsoukas cried at his dangling

organ and scrotum. "Exercise to make you lithe and flexible, put tone into your marrow!"

"You are a crazy sonofabitch," Caliope said. She had taken off her dress and sat on the edge of the bed in her slip, drawing off her stockings that were a maze of runs. He knew the movement of his naked body excited her and she could not help watching his gyrations.

"We are preparing, my friend and I," he said hoarsely. "You should be preparing as well."

"That's all you're good for," she said resentfully. She stood up and drew her black slip over her head. The flesh at her thighs and around her waist bulged against the ruptures of the worn girdle. "The stud," she said with a mocking laugh, and twisted her arms behind to unclasp her brassiere. As her heavy, dark-nippled breasts sagged free, she moaned and kneaded them gently with her fingers. "I need a new brassiere," she said. "The elastic on this one kills me."

"I will buy you two brassieres tomorrow," Matsoukas said.

"Yes, you will buy me two," Caliope said with a sharp grunt. "And maybe even a new dress and a new hat for Easter."

"I will buy you all these things!" he said. The blood had begun to move in his arms and a thin film of sweat spread across his shoulders and ran in trickles to his hairy armpits.

"I don't mind for myself anymore," she said. "But if my mother didn't buy the children the clothing they need, they would be in rags, and if she didn't pay most of the rent we would be in the street."

"Business is getting better," he said. "Expanded opportunities for me are in the stars." He drew a long deep breath. "We will repay your blessed mother so she can hide bigger piles of money under her mattress."

She stared at him for a moment with bitterness and wonder. Then she sighed and turned her back to him. She caught her fingers in the waist of her girdle and pulled it slowly down across her hips, a ripple of reddened flesh puffing in its wake. When it fell to her ankles she stepped out of it.

He watched her in that arc of his vision and her body seemed strangely distorted. She was slovenly and untidy, snail-like flakings of flesh marring her once solid hips and waist, her strong and firm buttocks grown to pouched and flabby folds. Yet her nakedness was desirable and he recalled with a mounting excitement the years of passion they had indulged, the wild humping journeys they had made.

With a buoyant cry he swung his feet back to the floor. He stood up breathing deeply, pleased at the racing of the blood through his limbs. He walked on bare feet to where she bent separating the clothing she had removed. He slipped his arm around her waist and caressed the nipple of her breast.

She twisted out of his grasp. Her lips were dry and hard.

"I'm tired," she said.

"I will refresh you," he said with a wink.

He reached for her again and she moved quickly back, her breasts jumping slightly toward him. With a smile of elation he moved forward and caught her. He stroked her shoulder and the hollow of her throat. She held herself taut and as he bent to kiss her breast she pushed him away.

"I want you, my darling," he said, and the scents of her body rose to tingle in his nose, something sour and moist with the tang of a dill pickle.

"I don't want you!" She struggled to break free. He felt her nails across the surface of his flesh and he tensed, waiting for them to pierce his skin. But they probed as if first seeking his veins before they stabbed him. He tried to pull her closer and she twisted from side to side denying him her sullen mouth. He stroked her arms with the balls of his thumbs, ran his fingers over her elbows down her wrists and then vaulted to the arched hills of her hips. He felt her suddenly go limp.

"Get it over with," she said.

"I don't want to get it over with," he protested.

"What the hell do you want?" she said savagely. "Do you want me a virgin again the way I was when you married me? Do you want me to bleed and cry once more for the wonder of love? That was three kids and four miscarriages ago. You can go to hell!"

He stepped back, releasing her, and studied her with a slight frown.

"What a Madonna you are," he said in a soft mocking voice. "You can freeze a man's cock with a few saintly words from your delicate mouth."

She watched him for a moment, breathing hard, the checked pattern of the girdle still visibly stitched across her belly.

"I wasn't always like that," she said. "Ten years with you has made me what I am."

"Don't give me all the credit, old dear," he smiled. "I see much of your mother's incomparable nature in you."

"You resent her because without her we would starve!"

He pointed to the folds of flesh around her waist. "You hardly seem to be wasting away," he smirked.

For a moment she seemed on the verge of cursing him and then she paused. A slight teasing smile, a parody of passion, glittered around her mouth. She made a small thrusting movement with her belly.

He leaped to pull her fiercely against his body. She offered him her mouth and he saw her red tongue glistening like a dagger between her lips. For an instant she appeared to yield and then in a swift rancorous movement she drove downward with her fingers. He felt an explosion of pain at his loins.

He let loose a tight anguished cry and grabbed for his stinging crotch. She twisted away from him, laughing hoarsely, her breasts swinging vengefully free.

"My passionate Greek God!" she hissed. "My Adonis who loves to canter up a spread-eagled pair of legs!"

"You harlot!" he cried. He was torn between pain and delight at her spirited violence. He could not endure her inertia and scorn.

"Someday I will fix you good!" she said. "I'll catch your big balls asleep and convert you from a stud into a gelding!"

"You would die without me to dip you!" he said. He took a menacing step toward her.

She retreated to the bed, shaking her head, climbing on it to kneel warily, half-teasing and partly in fear. The sight of her naked and trembling filled him with a wild horn of desire. He grabbed for her with a cry and jerked his hand aside just in time to evade the sharp bite of her teeth. He caught her thighs between his palms and roughly swung her big strong body down on the mattress. "Got you now!" he cried. "Now you'll get a pounding that will tame you!"

"Goddam you, let me go!" She struggled and kicked in fury, her hair fallen wild across her cheeks, her teeth bared in a snarl.

He held her down, forcing his face into the hollow of her throat, her body thrashing beneath him. For a few wild moments they struggled while he made her feel the urgent weight of his flesh. "Let me go," she said more quietly and he felt the wound of her anger healing. "You bastard, let me go."

He released her and she made no effort to rise. He bent and kissed her, mouth nuzzling and nipping at the taste of despair, his hands deftly herding the swells and folds of her body. Her arms tightened around his neck, her fingers pinched in a frenzied urgency at his flesh.

"You bastard," she cried softly, "O you bastard." But all fury and scorn were gone from her voice and a strange tender sorrow in its place. For an instant their faces were close and he watched her eyes, watched each tremor that swept the ridges of her cheeks until like thin sheer layers of crust the bitterness and hate were peeled away. He cried out wordlessly then at what appeared in her eyes, for one fleeting moment retrieved from the debris of the years, the warm shaken glitter of love.

Long after she had fallen asleep, snoring in a weary drawing of breath, he lay awake staring at the reflections of light within the frame of the window. The shrill laughter of a woman erupted from the street below, and a man joined her with a growl of mirth. Then a moment of silence broken by the lonely sound of a ship baying from the harbor of the river. A drunk stumbled noisily past, a tuneless melody rising garbled from his throat. The sound was lost in a rumble that stirred the air. It grew in volume until it burst outside the window and the elevated rocked by, framed glittering squares of light with a few heads like small black balls.

When it was quiet again a shimmer of moonlight breaking from the mooring of a cloud rippled over the sill, illuminating a worn patch of rug, the dresser, his clothes flung across a chair. Moonlight reached the bed, swept the blanketed swell of their bodies, a brief plume in which he saw Caliope's face through a veil of mist.

He thought of the moonlight threading the bars of Stavros' bed and he rose. He walked naked to the parlor, following the faint trail of moonlight to his son's bed.

The boy lay on his side, his legs drawn toward his stomach, his hands curled around his knees. His head was flung back on the pillow, his mouth was open and each breath wracked his body.

Matsoukas placed his fingers against the boy's throat, tracing the uneven fluttering of breath through the moist thin canal. He squatted on the floor and leaned his head gently against the bars.

"We will go there soon, you and I," he whispered. "You will lie naked in the sun on a high rock above the sea. The sun will make you well, will burn away your weakness with its healing fire. Soon, my son, soon."

His voice rose slightly and Stavros stirred in his sleep. Jubilantly it seemed to Matsoukas as if he had heard and understood for there was a radiance on his face, a light across his cheeks, a kind of joy that his body could not contain.

CHAPTER FIVE

ATSOUKAS walked brusquely beneath the sign that read, ATHEN AN LU CH, EVE YBO Y WE COME, pausing only an instant to examine fitfully the dilapidated exterior of the lunchroom. The perimeter of wood around the window revealing a maze of cracks. The lettering on the glass ragged and with half the letters chipped away. He shook his head and entered the doorway. The interior fully matched the exterior decorations. The battered pie case, the dented and tarnished coffee urns, the worn counter, the tables with faded and stained cloths cast a pall of wretchedness from wall to wall.

"Where are all the bloody customers?" Matsoukas asked loudly. "Has the city been evacuated? Is there no sign of life?"

Javaras, the owner of the lunchroom, came slowly from the kitchen. He was a tall thin man in his late fifties with a dark and mournful face. He smelled of rancid cheese, coffee grounds, stale bread, and disaster. He walked staring uneasily at the floor as if expecting it to collapse with his next step.

"The place is a graveyard," Javaras said grimly. "Who

60

are we fooling? When the prospective buyer gets here this afternoon the only way we will sell is to subdivide it into cemetery lots."

"Success in any endeavor is a benefit to be won, old sport," Matsoukas said. "Do not throw in your stained towel. We may yet turn this enterprise of your enslavement into the instrument of our liberation."

Uncle Louie, the chef, came to stand in the doorway from the kitchen. He was a shriveled and bowlegged grasshopper of a man with a high grease-riddled chef's cap perched crookedly on his head and a face like an embalmer's model.

"I am ashamed of both of you!" Matsoukas cried. "I expected to find the place gleaming with high polish and both of you quivering with anticipation. In less than two hours the redoubtable broker, Aristotle, will be here with the buyer we are both after. We should be bristling with confidence and instead your demeanors suggest a wake."

"We are out of eggs," Uncle Louie said in a grieved voice. "Apollo won't go after a dozen."

From the kitchen the shrill voice of Apollo responded, his shaggy head visible through the chute opening above his sink. "I am a dishwasher!" he cried. "Not a rutting errand boy!"

Javaras ignored them both. "What happened at the Union Hall?" he asked Matsoukas.

"Complete victory!" Matsoukas said gleefully. "I told my friend, Local 77 Vice President Orchowski that all afternoon today, coffee, sweetrolls, and ham sandwiches are free in the Athenian Lunch. The men who enter will pay and you will carefully give each one the little white cash register receipts. These receipts will be turned in to

Orchowski and you will reimburse the Union Recreation Fund for the amount of their total. In return Orchowski promises to keep this place packed all afternoon." He turned toward Uncle Louie. "Did you bake the ham?"

Uncle Louie nodded. "A twenty-two pounder all set," he said. "Just in time too. The meatman severed our credit this morning."

"And sweetrolls?" Matsoukas asked.

"Two hundred and twenty-five along with thirty loaves of bread," Javaras said. "Only two days old and I got them all at a good discount." He paused. "I just filled both five gallon urns with fresh coffee."

"We better get some eggs," Uncle Louie said.

"Go lay some!" Apollo cried from the kitchen.

"You better shut your face!" Uncle Louie cried wrathfully.

"We are all under a strain," Matsoukas said soothingly. "But we must remain calm. The secret of victory lies in proper organization and our planning has been extraordinary."

"I don't like it," Javaras said. "It's risky and dishonest too."

"Life is risky," Matsoukas said, "and as for business, old sport, it thrives on dishonesty. Do you realize at this very moment that paragon of dishonesty, that bloody real estate swindler, Aristotle, is trying to unload a restaurant deader than yours on the buyer? That pigeon is going to get plucked. The only question is whether Aristotle or I do the plucking. And the stakes are high. If we pull off this sale you are free after five years of bondage and I," he paused and a flush of heat swept his cheeks, "I will fly my son to Greece!"

They were silent for a moment watching him. He snapped his fingers. "Let us prepare now," he said. "Polish that abominable pie case and sweep the cursed floor. Find a fresh apron and a clean cap. We must move as the great Pindar counseled, to the swift movement and the strong beat of life itself!"

After a brief flurry of regular customers at lunch, the counters emptied again. Only a stray patron came in for coffee. Matsoukas waited just inside the front door staring anxiously at the street. Javaras stood nervously behind the cash register. Uncle Louie and Apollo bickered with one another to pass the time.

"Where are the union boys?" Javaras asked. "It won't look good if the buyer finds the place empty."

"Patience, man," Matsoukas said. "I told Orchowski to start sending his boys in after two. What good are patrons before the buyer arrives?" He stiffened suddenly. "Here comes the pigeon now!"

On the street outside the lunchroom appeared the broker, Aristotle, a heavy-jowled man in a checkered vest with a large gold watch chain suspended over his huge belly. The buyer was small and dapper with a wide-brimmed Borsalino set carefully on his head. Aristotle held him tightly by the arm. The broker pointed out the shabby exterior.

"Look at the well-fed wolf!" Matsoukas snarled over his shoulder to Javaras. "Trust that bloody stinknose to find cracks even the termites can't locate! I'm surprised he has the nerve to show his face after being fined last year for selling tickets to Greece on a steamship that didn't exist! Bloody crook!"

As they approached the door he burst into a hearty smile and pulled it open.

"Welcome!" he cried. "Come in gentlemen! Good to see you again, Aristotle, my dear friend!"

The broker and buyer entered the lunchroom, the buyer taking a final apprehensive look at the wretched window frame. Under the expensive hat he wore thick-lensed spectacles and through them his eyes became large magnified spheres.

"How are you, Matsoukas?" Aristotle said, his tone indicating he couldn't care less. "Mr. Cascabouris, this is Mr. Matsoukas," he paused to give the proper weight to his following words. "Broker for the seller."

"Delighted, sir!" Matsoukas shook the buyer's hand warmly. He motioned for Javaras to approach. "This is Mr. Javaras, a compatriot, and a restaurant man for thirty years. Mr. Javaras, allow me to present to you Mr. Casca-bouris, and my distinguished colleague, Aristotle, a man with a reputation equally venerated on land and on sea."

Aristotle coughed and blinked and fingered his heavy gold chain.

"Why do you wish to sell, Mr. Javaras?" Cascabouris asked bluntly.

"Frankly, I am tired," Javaras said. "I need a rest."

Aristotle looked around the lunchroom empty but for a single customer lounging over a cup of coffee. "Put a bed in that corner," he said. "You should not be disturbed." He chuckled as if relishing his wit.

"Men are like bells," Matsoukas said loudly. "You cannot tell which ones are cracked until they ring."

They all stared at him slightly puzzled and he motioned to one of the tables with four chairs. "We will make a rapid tour of the facilities first," he said, "and then return to the table there to watch the trade. Customers are what is important. Fixtures can be rebuilt, repainted, renovated."

"These fixtures look like they should be burned," Aristotle said. He made a desultory gesture of apology to Javaras. "No offense."

"I cannot afford a match," Javaras said grimly.

Matsoukas threw him a look of dismay. "Always kidding!" he cried. "I don't think Mr. Javaras fully appreciates what a wit he has! Cannot afford a match indeed!" He winked slyly at Cascabouris.

"Let me take your hat, sir," he said.

"He might as well keep it on," Aristotle said. "We won't be staying very long." He looked around. "Besides it might get soiled." He fluttered his fingers again at Javaras. "No offense."

Matsoukas gritted his teeth and led them through the swinging door into the dark and gloomy kitchen.

"Notice how spacious and roomy the icebox is," he said. "The stove appears a little worn but it is still in grand condition. They don't build them of cast iron like that anymore."

"They haven't since the Civil War," Aristotle smirked and nudged Cascabouris.

Matsoukas winced slightly under the barb and then, recovering quickly, introduced them to the chef. Uncle Louie nodded nervously and offered both of them his cold limp hand after wiping it furiously on his apron.

"And that is our dishwasher, Apollo," Matsoukas pointed to the shaggy-haired man at the sinks. "He has lost four assistants in the past month because of the frenzied activity but he remains undaunted and carries on alone!"

Apollo glowered at them and pulled up his pants which were held around his waist by a length of rope.

As Aristotle and Cascabouris passed out of the kitchen Uncle Louie motioned to Matsoukas. "We need eggs," he whispered.

Matsoukas waved him a hasty reassurance and followed the others out of the kitchen. Javaras waited with a wretched and forlorn look as if he expected they would head straight for the front door.

"It has been a long time," Aristotle said gravely, "since I have seen a place so ripe for total demolition. I would not trade this entire establishment for a three-wheeled pushcart." He shrugged again at Javaras. "No offense."

"A Greek businessman is not fooled by appearances," Matsoukas said grimly. "He knows well that many a flashy stainless steel surface conceals a cemetery vault. Isn't that right, Mr. Cascabouris?"

Cascabouris nodded sagely and Matsoukas held his chair. He gave him a slight push toward the table.

"Coffee for these gentlemen," he waved briskly at Javaras. "Perhaps a ham sandwich?"

"Just coffee," Cascabouris said.

Aristotle sat down with a poignant sigh suggesting the whole affair was a waste of time. Javaras brought the coffee and nervously sloshed some into the saucers. Matsoukas gave him a warning look.

The first group of union customers arrived, a half dozen express handlers in leather jackets. They sat in a boisterous group along the counter and ordered coffee and rolls. One buffoon ordered four ham sandwiches to go. Javaras glared at him but complied to avoid any disturbance. To each

66

man leaving, the owner was careful to hand out the small white register receipt.

"Mr. Javaras has to be extremely careful in recording his receipts," Matsoukas whispered to Cascabouris. "The income he derives from this incredible business makes him a joyous target for the Internal Revenue agents."

Aristotle grunted and drew his gold watch slowly and with ceremony from his vest pocket. Cascabouris raised his eyebrows silently showing he was suspending judgment.

A tumult at the door attracted their attention. About a dozen men were trying to enter at once, jamming the doorway. Javaras stared at them incredulously. Matsoukas knew there had not been that many people in the lunchroom since the afternoon a rumor had gone around the neighborhood that Uncle Louie was a bookie. The men filled almost all of the counter stools.

Matsoukas made a resigned gesture with his hands. "All day it goes like this," he said to Cascabouris. Aristotle frowned.

Javaras moved swiftly to take their orders. Coffee and sweet rolls. Coffee and ham sandwiches. One man asked for a lamb chop but he must have felt the dry heat shake off the owner's cheeks. He quickly changed his order to coffee.

Before this group had been fully served another half-dozen men entered, closely followed by what appeared to be the entire membership of Local 77. In a flash every stool and chair in the lunchroom was occupied.

"Uncle Louie! Apollo!" Javaras shouted. "On guard!"

Cascabouris looked at Aristotle and Matsoukas could see he was impressed. He reached up and slowly removed

67

his hat. "Perhaps we should watch from the kitchen," he said to Matsoukas. "It is not proper to occupy tables when customers are waiting."

"I commend your good judgment," Matsoukas said cheerfully. "As a restaurant man yourself you know every chair must pay its way."

He led them into the kitchen where they stood peering through the porthole of the door, the little buyer straining on his toes. The first load of soiled cups and saucers came down the chute into the sink and splattered the startled Apollo with water.

"What the hell...!" he said.

"Coffee!" Javaras shouted from the front. "Louie, ten ham sandwiches! Sweet rolls on eight!"

Uncle Louie was feverishly piling ham sandwiches on a large tray mumbling to himself. Javaras ran around frantically assembling sweet rolls and pouring coffee.

"I think I had best assist them," Matsoukas said to Cascabouris. "The regular waitress is ill today." He removed his suitcoat and hung it carefully over the back of a chair. He rolled up his sleeves and tied a clean apron around his waist, humming to himself.

"I'll take that tray of sandwiches out front," Matsoukas said to Uncle Louie. He picked up the tray and with a final broad grin at Aristotle, he moved swiftly into the fray.

He poured an endless stream of coffee and swept countless sweet rolls onto napkins. Javaras, bathed in sweat, made another urn of coffee, splashing the grounds over his apron in his wild haste. Still the door banged open and more men piled in. There was no place to sit and

68

they stood three deep behind the stools and chairs waiting for the occupants to finish.

"Twenty ham sandwiches!" Matsoukas shouted. "Nine sweet rolls! Fifteen coffees!"

Uncle Louie came from the kitchen with a massive tray of ham sandwiches piled in tiers. He staggered under the load and by the time he got to the coffee urns, they were all gone. Men reached over the counter to snatch them off the tray. More men appeared outside and when they could not enter because of the jam at the door stood peering fretfully through the glass. The men leaving had to push their way out.

Matsoukas rushed to the kitchen for more cups and saucers pausing an instant to smile warmly at the broker and Cascabouris who stood watching the turmoil in amazement. Cascabouris said nothing but behind the thick lenses of his glasses his eyes darted like fish in a bowl.

In the corner Apollo had his head bent almost into the suds, his arms and hands working like a frantic swimmer trying to keep from being drowned.

"More cups and saucers!" Matsoukas shouted at him. "Put a move on, man!"

Apollo raised his head dripping with suds and water. His lips trembled. "What the hell...!"

Uncle Louie clutched Matsoukas by the arm in panic. "I have an order for two fried eggs!" he gasped. "I told you!"

"Compose yourself!" Matsoukas cried. "Tell him the bloody hen is sulking!"

He rushed back toward the swinging door and Aristotle and Cascabouris moved quickly out of his way.

"A little quieter than usual today," Matsoukas said with a breathless smile. He pushed against the door and it would not give. He pushed harder and when he finally shoved with all his strength the door sprang open scattering the half-dozen men who had been pressed against the other side.

In the next ten minutes two police cars drove up with screaming sirens. When the policemen assured themselves there was no riot in progress they set up orderly lines along the sidewalk and directed traffic in and out of the lunchroom.

"Coffee!" Javaras shouted hoarsely handing out the white register receipts as fast as he could bang out the amounts. "Sweet rolls! Ham sandwiches! Cups! Saucers!"

"Ham is gone!" Uncle Louie cried shrilly from the kitchen. "I have a little salami! No eggs!"

"Salami sandwiches!" Matsoukas shouted. He was drenched in sweat, his shirt glued to his back, his apron stained with nuts, raisins, and coffee. On his next trip into the kitchen he paused to grin at the broker and buyer.

"Incredible," Aristotle said in a stunned voice. His cheeks quivered like a man caught in the grip of a nightmare. Cascabouris made his cross. "Police to direct the traffic!" he marveled. "Fantastic!"

Things quieted down slightly after that. When word spread that the lunchroom contained nothing besides toothpicks and water the crowd lined up outside dispersed grumbling. The tables and stools began to empty.

Uncle Louie had collapsed across a chair, his face beet-red, his hand pressed against his heart as if he feared a stroke. Apollo had locked himself in the toilet. Matsoukas bent over the sink washing his face and then dried his hands. He slipped back into his coat and walked jubilantly toward the buyer as Javaras came into the kitchen. For the first time in thirty years there was a fragment of hope on the owner's doleful face.

"Well," Javaras said to them all, and paused to get his breath. "What do you think?"

"Incredible," Aristotle shook his head sorrowfully.

Cascabouris moved quickly then and raised his arms and stretched on his toes to embrace Javaras around the shoulders. "Magnificent!" he said with emotion. He turned to Matsoukas and nodded fervently with a trace of tears in his eyes. "Magnificent! Simply magnificent!"

"You like it, eh?" Javaras said. He seemed on the verge of tears himself.

"Mr. Javaras," Cascabouris said in a trembling voice. "Permit me to extend to you my felicitations. Twenty-five years in the business myself, ten different locations, big restaurants and small lunchrooms and I swear to you I have never witnessed activity such as this. In a year a man could make a fortune."

"Right!" Matsoukas cried. "That is only the truth!" He threw a look of triumph at the grieving Aristotle.

"Thank you," Javaras said softly. "Thank you." He looked numbly at the floor, at the tips of his worn shoes.

"We can discuss an offer at once," Matsoukas said. "Mr. Javaras has made his money here. He is prepared to let the business go at a price covering his investment and a small profit. A contract can be drawn and signed in a few moments."

Cascabouris raised his hand. He smiled warmly. "I can-

71

not tell you how impressed I am," he said. "I know that nothing else I see can possibly equal this Homeric activity. But . . ." he paused. "I am no longer a young man. My heart flutters. In a year a man could make a fortune, true, but in three months I would be dead. This kind of activity might even kill me sooner."

A dreadful silence followed the buyer's words. Javaras staggered as if he had been kicked in the groin. Matsoukas stifled a fearful moan. Hope sprang like a flower to Aristotle's graveled cheeks.

"Mr. Cascabouris!" Matsoukas cried. "Do not be hasty! It is not always as vigorous as it was today! Sometimes it is very quiet! An hour, two, and maybe three go by and not one patron enters!" He nodded fiercely at Javaras who stared at him in horror and then began numbly to nod in unison with him.

"The truth," Javaras said hoarsely. "Often it is much quieter than today, much quieter. I swear it."

Cascabouris shook his head vigorously. "You are modest, Mr. Javaras," he said. "Don't be. Your spirit and energy have built this fantastic business. This is your testament, a shining example for every restaurant man in this great country. I will never forget I have been witness to a colossal and moving experience. Goodby, my friends, goodby."

He started through the swinging door and Aristotle leaped to follow his spoor. "I think you might reconsider that little jewel on 39th Street . . ." His voice faded and they walked out the front door with the broker's fingers working in earnest and furious patterns. Matsoukas watched them go.

Javaras flexed his arm slowly. First one arm and then the other as if he were testing his circulation. Uncle Louie came to stand beside them, his face swept by exhaustion.

"Are they coming back?" Uncle Louie asked.

"What is my faith?" Matsoukas said somberly. "To admit what is. What is, is catastrophe."

A single truck driver entered and sat down on a stool. Javaras opened the swinging door wide enough to put out his head.

"Ham sandwich and coffee," the man said.

"We are closed," Javaras shook his head. "There has been a death in the family." He waved the man farewell.

"Whose death?" Uncle Louie asked.

"Mine," Javaras said. "Very soon."

Apollo came out of the toilet and stood a moment staring at the mountain of dishes that engulfed the sinks. "What the hell . . .!" he cried and turned and went back into the toilet. They heard him snap the lock.

"Ye mortal men, resign yourselves," Matsoukas said. "The world to destiny belongs." He uttered a sigh that swept from deep in his bowels and then he straightened his shoulders and violently threw off the cape of gloom. "Do not despair, my friend," he said to Javaras. "Every disaster opens a perspective on the human condition. The true mettle of a man is revealed in his response to what seems to be defeat." He started through the swinging door.

"Where are you going?" Javaras asked.

Matsoukas paused.

"I go to the offices of Local 77," he said gravely. "Perhaps we can salvage something from this debacle. Perhaps my friend, Orchowski, will allow us to settle for twenty or twenty-five cents on the dollar. I will try."

"I expect nothing," Javaras said mournfully, "and will receive less."

"If you come back this way bring some eggs," Uncle Louie said.

CHAPTER SIX

I HAVE had it," Fatsas pushed himself away from the table into the perimeter of shadow. He looked disconsolately at the few worn dollar bills still before him. "I will keep this ragass stake until tonight."

"I join you," Charilaos said. "The faces of the cards begin to blur."

"We may as well stop," Matsoukas said. He leaned back and stretched his arms above his head in a great unjointing of his cramped limbs.

Carl, the dealer, who had been alternating with Cicero through the night nodded and assembled the cards to clear the table.

Matsoukas rose and walked to the corner where Cicero was asleep in an armchair. The dealer's small, spare body was bent in thin folds and his head hung limply to the side. In that phase of light he looked like a child. Matsoukas touched his shoulder gently. Cicero opened his eyes.

"Come on, old sport," Matsoukas said. "The night is over. I will walk you home."

He helped the dealer to his feet where he stood weaving

slightly and blinking his eyes. The odor of whiskey rose like damp pungent mist from his flesh. He grunted and nodded.

"I'll lock up," Carl said. "You go ahead."

Cicero gestured his thanks and braced slightly against Matsoukas, they followed the others to the door.

The four men stood for a moment in the alley outside the rear exit of the music store. The first gray stirrings of dawn had muted the glitter of stars leaving only a colorless firmament that swept their faces with an eerie light.

"What a bloody hour this is," Fatsas shivered. "Like the whole earth is a graveyard." He raised the collar of his coat and shrugged his head down like a turtle drawing into its shell. He shuffled off wearily. Charilaos waved a quick farewell and started on his way.

Matsoukas and Cicero walked the length of the alley. A solitary cat foraging among the garbage cans sighted them and leaped out of sight.

"One of my relatives," Cicero said. "My sister in Kenosha."

"I see a certain family resemblance," Matsoukas said.

They passed a darkened car and saw the shadowed outline of two bodies writhing in the rear seat.

"Can't the poor devils find a bed?" Matsoukas asked sadly.

"What's the difference where they do it?" Cicero said. He shivered and huddled slightly against Matsoukas for warmth. "Let's get a drink someplace," he said.

"You're going to sleep," Matsoukas said sternly. "You are about dead on your feet."

"That is my normal condition," Cicero said grimly. "Cold and almost dead."

"Hush, man," Matsoukas said. "You carry on and on." He embraced his friend around the small bony frame of his shoulders.

They emerged from the alley onto a street of shabby rooming houses. Before the stone steps of one of the houses Cicero turned and gestured a grave and courteous dismissal. "Thank you for the convoy, my friend," he said. "I will be fine from here."

Matsoukas gave him a slight shove. "Right into bed, old sport," he said. "The last time I left you here you were up the street in a flash."

"You are a scourge," Cicero sighed. He started wearily up the steps with Matsoukas holding his arm.

On the second floor they entered a long dark hallway. Cicero was breathing in short quick gasps. He fumbled with his key before his door until Matsoukas took it and found the lock. The door swung open on a dingy, cluttered room with an unmade bed. An assortment of books and soiled clothing littered the chairs, the top of the old bureau, and the floor.

"Mt. Olympus," Cicero grinned crookedly. He began to pull off his clothing until, stripped to his underwear, he sat down on the edge of the bed. He grunted and pulled a book from beneath his buttocks. His thin bare legs were lean as sticks and covered with a sparse coating of lank hair. He motioned toward the bureau.

"Matsoukas, be a sport," he pleaded. "Bring the bottle from the top drawer. I need a nightcap."

Matsoukas sighed and went to the dresser. He opened the drawer and carried the pint he found back to the bed. Cicero uncorked the bottle eagerly and threw back his head to take a long fervent swallow of the whiskey. He

77

breathed with renewed zest. He corked the bottle and started to slip it deftly beneath his pillow.

"No you don't!" Matsoukas snapped the bottle from his fingers. "The top drawer is close enough. Now get under the covers or I will crown you with it."

Cicero laughed and fell back across the bed, his body lying lightly upon the springs, his legs dangling over the edge. Matsoukas scooped him up easily and swung him into bed and then pulled the sheet and cover to his throat.

Cicero stared at the ceiling for a moment and then looked soddenly at Matsoukas.

"Why do you bother with me?" he asked.

"Because you are a man of rare soul," Matsoukas said. "A man I delight in calling my best friend."

Cicero shook his head slowly. "Friendship blinds you," he said. "If you could see me as clearly as I see myself, you would know what I am. A frail-bodied drunk with a groaning liver and a moaning heart. My veins are scurvy roads that run through the ruins of my body. I am a clown, a coward, a weakling, and a fool."

"No!" Matsoukas cried in heated protest.

"A wrecked ship that even in its prime was never seaworthy," Cicero said, "never worth a damn, never fit for floating except in a muddy gutter swollen with the vomit of swine."

"You are mad!" Matsoukas cried. "The booze has soaked your head." He snorted. "Just your hands alone, those marvelous fingers ... they alone give you a kind of grace denied ordinary men."

Cicero shook his head with a slight smile tickling the corners of his lips. "Tell me again," he said. "Tell me your weird visions again. I have heard them many times and yet I take a strange perverse delight in hearing you tell me again."

Matsoukas winked at his friend. "Laugh and sneer if you wish," he said. He motioned to the scattered books. "You cannot conceal the truth of what you are from me. I know you too well. You are ten times the scholar that I am. You could write essays and poems. The world would acclaim you." He paused and shook his head gravely. "If you had lived in the golden age," he said, "you might have been a Praxiteles fashioning marvelous figures from marble, gorgons and heroes, and warriors and poets."

He fell silent and for a moment they stared at one another. Resting in the cradle of the pillow the dealer's white cheeks glittered beneath the dark pits of his eyes. Matsoukas rose and straightened the covers once more around his throat.

"You care for me like my mother used to do," Cicero said with a soft mocking melancholia in his voice. "Tuck me in and hear my prayers." He closed his eyes and began to intone in a faint thin voice.

> Now, dear God, I go to bed
> And rest my little weary head.
> When daylight comes please let me rise
> To play once more beneath your skies.

He opened his eyes and stared with a strange burning sadness at Matsoukas. "The sun is only young once," he said. Then he closed his eyes again.

Matsoukas sat on the edge of the bed. He saw the outline of the dealer's fingers beneath the covers and he extended his own hand to shield them. He pressed gently and Cicero smiled slightly, his head slipping more deeply into the pillow. In a moment he was asleep, his breath coming in short uneven spasms.

Matsoukas rose quietly and looked down at his friend. "The sun is eternal," he said softly. Then a bone-piercing weariness crept the length of his body and he yearned suddenly for the warmth of his own bed.

He left the room and descended to the street. With his head bent to protect his weary eyes against the growing light he walked home quickly. He entered his building, and on the landing outside his door a baby's wail from a nearby flat cut sharply across the stillness. He put his fingers to his lips in a mute plea. He removed his shoes, swung the door open quietly, and walked in on stockinged feet. He paused in the parlor to peer down at Stavros and gently raised the blanket to the boy's throat.

He undressed outside the door of his bedroom. When he was naked he entered the room and walked on his toes to the bed. He pulled aside the covers and slipped stealthily beneath them trying not to waken Caliope who was snoring slightly. In the warmth of the bed he let his body relax and could have groaned with delight for the sheer sensual pleasure it provided him. He turned on his side and prodded with his rump until he found the curve of Caliope's buttocks. He pressed his body against hers, a touch without desire, seeking only the wellsprings of warmth.

He fell asleep and had a dream he was lying in a grave, an open grave of incredible depth, the sky above him reduced to a small square of light. Something stirred at the grave's edge and a voice called to him, a summons

80

from a great distance that fell slowly toward him and finally reached him like a distant echo. He struggled to answer the summons and the voice burst again close to his head. His eyes tore open to Faith crouched beside the bed, her small wet mouth close to his ear, her breath warm upon his cheek. He fumbled one arm out to stroke her hair and with the other hand groped to find the bed beside him empty.

"We are all going to church, Papa," Faith said. "The Bishop will be there today. Mama wants to take Stavros. Will you come with us?"

He groaned. "Tell Mama I am coming," he tried to sound alert. "Tell her to wait for me, that I will carry him, and not to put him in that cursed buggy."

Faith left the room and he struggled to break free of his blankets. He tugged desperately and managed to prop himself on one elbow and swing one naked leg almost to the floor. His big bare foot dangled a few inches above the wood. For a moment he studied it somberly, feeling it disembodied, a part of him severed from the remainder of his body. It swayed slightly and his eyes followed the swaying and he counted the toes. When he came to six he was startled and began to count again and the foot kept swaying . . .

He woke to a dreadful silence. His eyelids snapped open, his ears quivered, and he lay fervently still listening for some voice or movement around him.

"God curse me!" he cried and kicked off the covers and ran naked to the bedroom door. He stuck his head out into the hall.

"Caliope!" he shouted.

Even as his voice echoed through the deserted rooms

he understood she had scorned to send to wake him a second time. He had a fearful vision of her pushing the heavy reinforced buggy of Stavros through the streets, her mother and Faith and Hope grumbling and fretting at each corner as she made the lurching descents and straining ascents over the curbs.

He flung on his clothes in haste. He hurried down the stairs and ran the four blocks to the Orthodox church on Washtenaw, loping along with long easy strides, feeling the blood rise and tingle in his body.

When he reached the church a few young men lounged on the stone steps outside, smoking cigarettes, and waiting for the liturgy to finish. They giggled at the sight of Matsoukas, a fool so eager to get into church he had to run.

"Take it easy, pop," one youth with pustules the size of grapes called out smirkingly. "Jesus Christ won't let them finish without you."

Matsoukas considered pausing to slap his sassy mouth but could not spare the time. He pulled open the carved wooden door and entered the portico. Stavros' buggy was standing empty in the corner, the wide strong straps they used to bind him in hanging over the arms. Matsoukas started to enter the nave, the main part of the church, and the trustee behind the candle counter coughed to remind him he had neglected the amenities.

Matsoukas dropped a few small coins into the tray and the man smiled. Afterwards he lit a candle hastily, made his cross before the icon and entered the incense-misted church.

The congregation, under the great chandeliers which represented the stars in the sky and the Heavenly Light that God sends down, were clustered thickly in the benches at the front and sparsely in the rear. The old white-haired parish priest, Father Uranos, was standing in his vestments with folded hands gazing resignedly up at the imposing figure of Bishop Zenoitis on the platform of the great Episcopal Throne.

Bishop Zenoitis was a stately stout man with expressive hands. From his round face a pair of dark almond eyes stared upon the parishioners with a stabbing glitter. His trim beard, like the chin tuft of a handsome goat, was black and well-brushed and quivered as he spoke.

"What is this curse of modern life I speak of?" Bishop Zenoitis said loudly. "This abomination that ranks beside the tax collector, the bikini, the cinema, the television, as one of the foul plagues of our horrendous age . . . what is this evil but . . ." His dark eyes curved across the benches with a blade of scorn. ". . . the life insurance policy!" he cried.

Matsoukas peered along the benches for a sight of his family. A number of men and women distracted momentarily from the Bishop's penetrating assault clamped their teeth at him in disapproval.

"Yes, the life insurance policy!" Bishop Zenoitis thundered. "Those loathsome certificates full of fine print that smear death with the grossest ribaldry, making widows secretly jubilant, impatient for death to call, 'Haul ho!' for the coffined remains of their husbands so they might claim the beneficiary!"

Matsoukas saw Caliope in a bench off the center aisle. He quickly circled the church, the only figure moving, walking up the center aisle. Caliope was sitting on the outside, Stavros braced stiffly against her body. The mother-in-law sat on the other side of him with Faith and Hope beside her.

Bishop Zenoitis paused and watched Matsoukas. He bent slightly forward, his teeth bared, speaking directly to the intruder.

"Did the wives of the warriors of 1821 receive insurance? Did those magnificent iron-beards rising to fight the murderous Turk pause first to make sure their insurance premiums were paid?"

Matsoukas touched Caliope's shoulder and she raised her head to rend him with a grim and condemning look. He slipped past her and motioned to the old dragon to move so he might sit beside Stavros. She gave him a silent snarl, false teeth flashing in a harness of withered gums, and reluctantly shifted her bony rump a few grudging inches. Matsoukas bumped the end of the footrest, knocking it from the rack to the floor. The noise resounded like a boom of cannon fire through the church. Faith and Hope giggled and the Bishop glared at them in a fierce rebuke. Matsoukas waved him a quick apology and sat down beside Stavros. A segment of his hard heavy thigh mashed the old lady's hip and she wrenched away with a harsh groan. He winked amiably at her and turned to his son.

Stavros stared at his father, small furrows forming above his brows. Then a quiver of warmth swept the cold circles of his face and he lurched toward him. Matsoukas cradled the boy's head in the hollow of his arm and shoulder. He blew lightly against the soft fine hair and when the boy stirred with pleasure, he kissed him gently on the tip of his ear.

"I exhort you, my fellow Christians!" Bishop Zenoitis cried. "Abandon life insurance! Return integrity to grief!

Burn the cursed policies and when you lose your loved ones, weep in earnest! How much more sincerely will you be able to grieve when you are not expecting a check for ten or twenty or even fifty thousand dollars!"

He ended on a sharply severed word and looked up toward the dome of the church as if expecting a personal sign of God's approbation. When nothing materialized he uttered a long sigh. "Amen," he said. He made a desultory sign of the cross over the congregation and descended from the throne. Father Uranos followed him to stand before the Beautiful Gate, and the golden scrolls and crosses on their gilded vestments glittered richly in the light of the myriad candles.

The black-gowned and white-collared girls of the choir rose from their chairs in the loft. When they were absolutely still, the choirmaster lowered his fingers in a slow descent and then swept them swiftly upward. The girl's voices burst from their bosoms and throats in the hymn of hosanna.

Bishop Zenoitis entered the Sanctuary and turned to face the benches. The congregation rose. Matsoukas got to his feet and swung Stavros gently up in his arms, to perch him like a prince on the throne of his shoulder. Then Matsoukas' heart caught in a great wrenching of delight.

Directly across the aisle, no more than half a dozen feet away, was Anthoula. She was clad in a black full-skirted dress and dark jacket, both serving to mute the beautiful valleys and slopes of her body. Her cheek and a section of long lovely throat were visible, a coil of dark hair fallen loose beneath the soft-brimmed hat that rippled about her head.

And suddenly standing there with his son in his arms,

he felt a fierce surge of heat through his body, desire so strong that he almost cried out. He had all he could do to refrain from putting Stavros down and leaping across the aisle to snatch up Anthoula in his arms, a maddened centaur abducting a Lapith bride.

With his eyes burning her, she stirred restlessly. She turned suddenly and looking past Caliope, found him. She stared at him and then at Stavros and Caliope, piecing together the family, and then back to him. A strangeness was in her face, wonder, and a glitter of fear. He did not understand how it had taken place but his disorder had transmitted itself to her core, a violent response in her blood to the turmoil in his veins. She looked back toward the Sanctuary but he saw the quiver that ran the length of her body and he was filled with a wild jubilation.

He felt Caliope staring at him and he tore his gaze from Anthoula. He concentrated with intensity upon the icon of St. Basil, gowned in a garland of virtue, censuring him for his lascivious soul. But within his body he felt himself reverberating as if his organs were drums and cymbals played upon by a trio of tympanists.

At the moment when the dissonance was at its shrillest, a new sound intruded, a weird scream that chilled the marrow of his bones. And in his arms Stavros seemed to break apart.

He caught the boy's body and held him tightly against the spasm that shattered his flesh. His eyes were small dark leaves caught in a fearful wind, his mouth open and strangely blue.

Matsoukas felt the whole of the church swaying toward them, a flashing pattern of darkness and light with the ripple of shaken coins. The Bishop's neck rose like the head of a startled crane. Father Uranos peered around the corner of a candelabra. The girls of the choir pressed toward the railing of the loft to hang with their white collars suspended over the abyss of the church. The hundreds of men and women twisted and stretched like a maze of roots torn loose from the trunk of the benches.

He pushed quickly into the aisle holding Stavros in his arms, feeling each frantic arc of the boy's ribs against his own chest. For an instant as he turned toward the rear of the church he saw Anthoula watching him, a shaken compassion in her cheeks.

When he reached the portico, one of the trustees motioned to a door at the side and then ran to open it. Matsoukas carried Stavros into a secretary's office containing desk, chair, and couch. He placed the boy down carefully on the pillows of the couch, holding the heaving body under the reins of his hands. The boy's harsh and terrible gasps went on, his flesh a cracked shell over the bones of his face.

The trustee stood at the foot of the couch, watching intently, until a silent savage warning look from Matsoukas drove him to the door. As he went out, Caliope entered, carrying a small woolen blanket. She was breathing rapidly and several strands of her dark hair had fallen loose and cut her cheeks like knives. While Matsoukas tried to hold the boy's head immobile she inserted the wadded corner of a towel into his mouth to hold down his tongue.

Now in the full eruption of the spasm, the sweat strung long tendrils of beads around the boy's face and throat. His nostrils flared and beneath his clothing his shoulders thrashed like the broken wings of some small crippled bird. Once when the boy's agony seemed too much for his

87

body to sustain, Matsoukas cried out savagely. Through the closed door floated the hymns and chants of the service.

The door opened and a doctor entered carrying his black bag. Caliope moved aside to let him approach the couch but for a long moment Matsoukas would not release his son. Only when Caliope tugged urgently at his shoulder did he lean back. Even as the doctor bent to examine Stavros, the peak of the seizure passed. The boy's face grew strangely and suddenly calm.

When the doctor turned to get something from his bag, Stavros looked up at Matsoukas with a sharp burning brightness, a lucidity and awareness beyond his usual grasp. In that momentary bounty for all the anguish, Matsoukas bent and kissed the boy's cold lips.

"How often do these seizures come?" the doctor asked.

"Last year he had six," Caliope said slowly.

"This year?"

She was silent a moment. "They come more often now," she said.

"How often?"

She looked at Matsoukas. He sat watching the boy.

"I think the last one was...I think about three weeks ago." She looked again at Matsoukas for confirmation, but he did not move.

The doctor started to speak and then faltered. He turned away closing his bag with a loud snap.

"Don't move him for a while," he said. "Let him rest and sleep right there for a few hours."

After the doctor left they sat silently watching the boy. He had drifted instantly into sleep, his breathing coming in short and even rhythm. The services had ended and the

88

rustle of people, the low rumble of voices, came from the other side of the door.

"You go home with the girls," Matsoukas said. "When he wakes I will carry him home. You take the buggy."

Caliope walked to the door and turned.

"Mama can take the girls home," she said quietly. "I can wait with you."

He did not answer. After a moment of silence she opened the door and went out.

He sat beside Stavros for a long time. The last voices faded from the portico and the church grew quiet. He pulled the blanket to the boy's throat and bent once to peer closely at his face. He placed the tip of his fingers upon the boy's chest and felt the faint flutter of his heart.

He heard a hesitant knock upon the door. After a moment it opened slightly and then slowly opened wider. The old priest, Father Uranos, entered. He had changed from his vestments and was dressed in a dark suit. His white collar gleamed around the thin frail bones of his throat. He stood uncertainly inside the door.

"How is the boy?" he asked.

"He is asleep," Matsoukas said. "He will be all right."

The priest walked softly to the couch and looked down upon the sleeping boy. He bent forward slightly.

"Don't touch him," Matsoukas said.

The priest straightened up and looked at Matsoukas. A strange melancholia swept his cheeks. He looked again at Stavros.

"Eternity is a great ring of light," he said quietly. "There is no suffering there. Suffering belongs to life."

"Death is darkness," Matsoukas said.

The priest walked slowly to the door. He hesitated with his hand upon the knob.

"I will pray for your son," he said.

Matsoukas did not answer. The priest left, closing the door quietly behind him.

Matsoukas sat for another few moments. Then unable to remain still any longer he rose and walked from the office leaving the door open. He passed through the portico and entered the church. He stood inhaling the last wisps of incense that lingered in the air.

He saw the church now as he had never seen it before, shadowed and emptied of people, a stage with the players gone and the dynamis of hymn and candle snuffed out.

He walked along the center aisle, the carpeting muffling his steps until he came to stand before the Sanctuary. The portals on either side were decorated by icons of the saints. Small oil lamps hung before each icon, double-wicked lamps burning the twin flames of the two natures of Christ, the human and the divine.

He pondered the desiccated arms, the austere faces, the inanimate hands of the figures in the icons. Flesh had been eaten from them by endless fast and prayer. When they finally died they could not have offered much of a repast for the maggots, the little flesh remaining on their bones expiring in frail puffs.

Within the Sanctuary stood the great altar table of marble. On the top of the table were the gospel-book, the candlesticks, and the ark for the sacrament of communion. Behind the altar loomed the crucifix, the large wooden cross on which a carved life-sized body of Christ was nailed. Above his head on the cross were the first letters for the words, "Jesus Nazarene, King of Jews," the inscription with which the soldiers mocked him on Golgotha.

He squatted on the floor before the entrance to the Sanctuary. He sat quietly staring toward the high white altar. The full firmament of the church, icons, crosses, candles, incense, and crucifix whirled about his head. He admitted them slowly and gravely into his soul. As the waning wax of the candle turns pliant, he felt his heart yielding.

"Are you really here?" he asked, and his words flew in soft echoes across the silent church. He bent forward slightly and listened. But the myriad angels did not waver, their fluted wings remained immobile, the heads of the saints masked within the shadows did not stir.

"Some say you are dead," he said, "that all this is mask and charade. I will tell you what I think has happened. Heaven has become for you a shadowed cavern of emptiness and longing. When Job asked, 'Why died I not from the womb?' you could still answer. But our earth is not the same as the earth on which Job lived."

The blue shades of the afternoon suddenly darkened. He looked up to the windows in the dome and saw them obscured under the passage of a dusking cloud. Shadows swept like suppliants across the empty pews.

"Once you could apportion heaven and hell," he said, "but that is true no longer. Error and chance rule the world. Your glory has departed."

He rose restlessly to his feet. He had a sense of floating toward stark hills wild with tangled shrubs and crevices, a peak on which a great mournful eagle perched.

"And they fill the churches and temples and pray to you," he said. "They light candles and beseech you to make the blind see, the crippled walk, the dead resurrected. They do not mark the trail of your blood."

A sound from the rear of the church drew him up tensely fearing that Stavros might have wakened. He started quickly down the aisle. At the doors to the portico he paused to look back a moment toward the Sanctuary. Then he raised his hand and slowly made the sign of the cross over the darkened church.

"Man have mercy on you," he said softly.

CHAPTER SEVEN

SILENT office before noon. Matsoukas waiting expectantly for clients. Anticipating an interruption momentarily he sat at his desk and carefully copied onto a tablet of clean white pages the ode "Olympia 2" of Pindar, savoring the swift strong beat of the measures.

> Beside the high gods
> they who had joy in keeping faith lead a life
> without tears. The rest look on a blank face
> of evil.

He recited the lines aloud as he dusted the frames and glass of his photographs, and declaimed the words ringingly as he admired his sculpture.

> ... winds sweep from the Ocean
> across the island of the Blessed.
> Gold flowers to flame
> on land in the glory of trees ...

He paused before the window and looked uneasily down at the door of the bakery. He had been unable to catch a glimpse of Anthoula during the entire morning and he feared she might be ill.

Since the hour in church several days before when he had felt her responding to his desire, he had been frantic in calculating how to approach her. But the cursed racks and counters of the bakery, like a medieval moat, and the hawk eye of old lady Barboonis, held him straining at bay.

To finance a trip to the bakery he turned his pockets inside out and from the deep core of lint and grains of tobacco mined a scatter of nickels and pennies. Ransacking the office he uncovered an additional dime in the rear of his desk drawer, lost beneath a sheaf of circulars and clippings of past performances from the Racing Form. A more exhaustive search failed to produce a penny more. To aggravate the situation he felt the ravages of hunger assaulting his belly and a thirst in his throat that could not be appeased with water.

He washed his hands and briskly brushed his hair. He retied his necktie to conceal an eggstain that blemished one of the loops. He opened the door of the office preparing to post the small printed sign which read,

EMERGENCY CALL
BACK IN 15 MINUTES

when he heard footsteps in the hall behind him.

He whipped the sign back into his pocket and turned eagerly around. A woman emerged from the shadows and with her a boy of about twelve or thirteen.

"Mr. Matsoukas?" she asked. She was in her late forties or early fifties, weary-cheeked with a tight and tired mouth. A faint and shredded remnant of youthful loveliness lingered only about her dark eyes.

"Yes, indeed," he smiled warmly. "Please come in."

She turned to the boy who stared at Matsoukas with

94

hostility and fear. "You wait here," she said. She gestured toward him. "My son, Tony," she said.

Matsoukas smiled a greeting, but the boy did not smile or speak. The woman entered the office and Matsoukas closed the door. She wore a worn cloth coat, frayed at the collar and the sleeves, heavy cotton stockings and flat-heeled black shoes.

"My name is Mrs. Cournos," she said. She looked toward the closed door and lowered her voice. "I came to you because Mrs. Ganas, a neighbor of mine, told me how you cured her son of bed wetting after the doctors could do nothing."

"Sit down, Mrs. Cournos," Matsoukas said.

She moved restlessly to a chair. "I am a waitress at the Cavalcade restaurant," she said, "and I have to hurry back." He saw her tighten slightly as she noticed the statuette of Aphrodite on his desk. She looked back to Matsoukas. "It's about my son," she said softly. "His father ... my husband, left us about seven years ago. I have a smaller daughter as well."

"I am sorry," Matsoukas said.

She shook her head, rejecting his solicitude. "I won't lie to you," she said. "I wasn't unhappy that he left even though it is a struggle to make ends meet. He beat me and beat the children. But now, for the first time, I miss him ... I miss him because the boy has reached an age where he needs a man to talk with, to counsel him about ... about life."

"I understand," Matsoukas said gently.

"I have tried to talk to him," she said helplessly. "But it needs a man to tell him these things. He has some knowledge from the streets, from the bad boys who curse and swear, but I think it is all mixed up." She paused and her voice fell to a barely audible whisper of distress. "The other night I walked into the bathroom, the lock on the door is broken, and he...he..." She stopped with a shame and wretchedness mantling her cheeks.

"Masturbation is common at his age," Matsoukas smiled to reassure her. "You want me to talk to him, to tell him these things about sex and life?"

She nodded silently.

"Then I will talk to him," Matsoukas said. "Don't worry. You go back to work and I will send him along when we are through."

She stood up, started slowly to the door, stopped and looked back at him. The pale tip of her tongue came out to lick her lips. "How much...?" she asked slowly. "How much will you charge?"

"A very small fee," Matsoukas shrugged. "This is no massive problem. A dollar or so."

She fumbled at the clasp of her purse.

"No need to pay me now," he said. "I will send you a statement on the first of next month."

He walked past her and opened the door. The boy stood where they had left him, his face pale in the shadows.

"This is Mr. Matsoukas," his mother said. "He will talk to you. Listen to him."

The boy barely nodded a frightened assent. His mother walked by, hesitated, and then slowly put out her hand to touch his arm in a kind of consolation. She looked back at Matsoukas in a trembling appeal and then turned and walked down the hall.

The boy looked once after his mother and Matsoukas saw him tense to cry out.

"What grade are you in school, Tony?" Matsoukas asked.

The boy turned back to him. He was slightly built with handsome dark eyes and straight black hair that fell in a lopsided bang across his forehead. He licked his lips in the same nervous gesture as his mother. Matsoukas swung the door open wider and motioned him to enter.

"Seventh," the boy said and slowly entered the office. Inside the door he stopped and licked his lips again. "Are you a doctor?" he asked and a whisper of terror lurked just beneath the words.

"Not a regular doctor," Matsoukas said. "A doctor of life."

He returned to the desk and busied himself with some papers. He made out he was reading a letter and studied the boy with slitted eyes. Tony shifted restlessly from one leg to the other, watching him, waiting. After several moments in which Matsoukas did not move or speak Tony began examining the office. His eyes found the naked Aphrodite and flared with panic as he tore his gaze away. He looked at Matsoukas and then sneaked another trembling look at the statuette. Matsoukas rustled the papers as a warning. When he looked up Tony was intently studying the silver-buckled belt on the corner of the desk.

"Hellenic Championship of Pittsburgh, 1947-1948," Matsoukas said. "I was twenty-seven then. I won that belt wrestling the mighty Zahundos, a steelworker built like a blast furnace. You ever heard of Zahundos?"

Tony shook his head.

"You are too young," Matsoukas said. "I tell you, boy, he was a terror. Nearly broke my back before I pinned him

97

for the deciding fall. We wrestled for almost three hours. The match had an hour time limit but neither of us had been able to pin the other and our blood was up. We wouldn't stop or accept a draw and they extended the time. I tell you that was a match to see."

The boy listened with his eyes intent on the belt.

"Do you wrestle?" Matsoukas asked.

The boy shook his head.

"You've got the build of a good wrestler," Matsoukas said somberly. "Not enough weight or muscle yet but you look fast on your feet and have good arms."

A tremor of pleasure glistened across the pale cheeks.

"Tell you what," Matsoukas said casually. "I'm going to teach you a few holds. None of that grunt and groan nonsense you see on television but some of the real stuff."

"You will?" the boy said and there was wonder and delight quivering just below the dark surface of his eyes.

"You come here and meet me tomorrow morning, Saturday," Matsoukas said, "and we'll go over to the Y.M.C.A. gym. I'll show you five or six good holds that will keep the bullies at bay. Bring along shorts and gym shoes."

"Is that why my mother brought me here?" the boy stared at him in disbelief.

"Of course," Matsoukas said brusquely. "What did you think? When you want lessons, you come to a champion."

The boy picked up the heavy belt with a slow careful reverence. He looked apprehensively at Matsoukas as if he should have asked permission first.

"That's all right," Matsoukas said. "Someday you may win one like it. I told you that you move like a wrestler. You walk with a fine loose swing to your body, a natural grace. Very few boys have it at your age."

98

Tony looked at Matsoukas thunderstruck. "I have it?"

Matsoukas made a gesture of impatience. "Would I tell you you had it if you didn't have it?" He looked at the small clock on his desk. "You had best get back to the restaurant," he said.

Tony nodded. "Saturday morning?" he asked again as if he could not believe it.

"Saturday morning," Matsoukas said.

Tony turned excitedly toward the door. When he put his hand on the knob, Matsoukas spoke again.

"Wait a minute," he said. "There are a few warming-up exercises. I'll show you one or two now so you can practice them for Saturday."

He motioned to Tony to stand across from him. He came from behind the desk.

"This is a good one," he said. Tony watched him intently. "You stand with feet apart and hands pressed, like this, against your thighs. You hold your hips steady and then you rotate your entire upper body in a circle, first to the right and then to the left, getting all the movement from back, sides, and front of the waist. You try it."

Tony began to rotate his body holding himself stiffly.

"Keep your feet apart," Matsoukas said. "Relax." He nodded with pleasure. "You're getting it. That's fine."

Tony smiled with a flashing glitter of teeth and began to rotate faster.

"Easy, easy!" Matsoukas cried. "You don't want to overdo it!"

Tony stopped, breathing hoarsely, grinning furiously.

"The next exercise we do on the floor," Matsoukas said. "We begin flat on the back, legs extended, arms at the sides . . ." He paused. "You should be wearing a supporter

99

for this one. All the wrestlers and gymnasts wear them."

Tony looked at him uncertainly.

"They call them jockstraps," Matsoukas said. "Hold's a man's organ and testicles so they won't get wrenched or bumped. That's important."

"I don't have one," the boy said with dismay darkening his cheeks.

"No problem," Matsoukas said. "They're inexpensive and we can pick one up on Saturday. You should have one. I had an accident when I was about your age. A friend of mine was teaching me to wrestle. I wasn't wearing a supporter and hurt myself right in the testicles."

"You did?"

"Right!" Matsoukas said. "Hurt like hell! The blessed organs are sensitive at that age, at your age. Do you know why?"

The boy shook his head slowly.

"Because that's the age when a boy's body begins to change into the body of a young man. The voice deepens, there is muscle coming to the arms, hair sprouts under the armpits, around the penis. It's a wonderful time."

Tony watched him, listening gravely, an uneasy distress returning to his cheeks and around his mouth.

"I'll never forget my father," Matsoukas said softly, "talking to me about the time I was your age. He took me aside one day and he told me, boy, I have seen you snickering and giggling with your cronies when you look at the cow and the bull. It's time you knew what life was really about." Matsoukas paused somberly. "Of course, that was in the old country. Over here boys your age already know all about this business of life."

He walked casually to the desk and sat on the edge,

crossing his arms, his head bent in studied recall.

"We walked in the fields," he said, "and my father told me about men and women. That maybe once, long ago, when the earth was very young, they were one. Somehow they were separated into the sexes we know today. But men and women spend their lives trying to find that part of them which they lost. That is why men look at women and why women look at men. When they find someone they long to touch, to embrace, then love is born." He paused to look sternly at the boy. "It has nothing to do with the stories you hear from friends, the smirks and leers, the crude drawings by morons on the toilet walls. It has to do with the most beautiful thing on earth, with love." The boy watched him in a strange breathless suspension. "With love the man feels his body coming alive," Matsoukas said. "He savors the moon and relishes the sun. He yearns to put his penis into the woman's nest, that sacred opening between her legs. In this way they are joined together in a kind of holy and mighty union. The grandest thing in the world, my father said, it shows you have found that which you had lost."

He moved from the side of the desk and laughed softly.

"I wondered how the man did this, when he did this," he said. "My father answered that all that knowledge would come in due time. A man does this when he marries, then he releases a seed inside of the woman, a seed of love. The woman nourishes this seed with her own blood and from it a baby is created and born. The way all of us are conceived. Poets and generals, beggars and kings. Simple stuff to you, boy, but all new to me."

Tony stared at him, his cheeks pale, his breath surging in small agitated movements from between his lips.

"And my father said to me," Matsoukas went on, "that all this marvel has its beginning at the age when the penis begins to stir. There are strange sensations, strange hot burnings. A boy becomes conscious of his organ in a way he has never been before, wants to touch it, pull at it, rub it."

The boy tensed. For a fleeting moment the harried panic and fear returned to his eyes. Matsoukas turned away and spoke quietly and casually.

"I confessed to my father that I had done this a number of times," he said, "had pulled at it and rubbed it until it stiffened and spurted off. You know what he told me then?" Matsoukas stared toward the paintings of the patriarchs on the wall. "Go ahead and do it, he said to me, do it a few times to see what it's like. Your grandfathers did it and I did it when I was your age. When you grow older you won't feel the need to do it anymore. But try it and understand that it's part of this wonderful second birth. It shows a boy that his body is gaining strength, that in a few years he will be bursting with power. It's like the clouds of childhood clearing away and the sun of manhood sweeping across the earth."

He paused again and slapped his leg in sudden exasperation. "Why do I waste time rehashing all this stuff for a bright boy like you?" he said. "You understand all this already, don't you?"

The boy could not meet his eyes and for a moment stared at the floor. Then he looked back at Matsoukas. He nodded slowly in a grave and quiet response.

"That's fine," Matsoukas said. "Now you better run along because I have a busy afternoon. See you tomorrow morning."

"Tomorrow morning," the boy said, and excitement flashed once more in his face, and a strange relief lightening the tight shadow of his cheeks. He turned and started quickly from the office. He opened the door and almost ran headlong into Cicero who stood startled in the doorway, a large brown paper bag clutched in his arms. The boy stumbled around him to continue down the hall.

"What a delightful surprise!" Matsoukas cried. "Come in, my friend!"

"Your clients are getting younger," Cicero grinned. "Is this one a bed wetter or isn't he weaned yet?"

"He wants to be a dealer," Matsoukas said. "I suggested he apprentice as a blacksmith."

Cicero laughed and entered the office. With a roguish raising of his brows he indicated the bag he held in his arms. He deposited it carefully on the desk while Matsoukas held his breath in anticipation.

"A loaf of lagana!" Cicero brought it out of the bag. "Wonderful!"

"A pound of feta!" Cicero said.

"Delightful!"

"And then . . ." Cicero paused suspensefully. "Wine!" he drew out a bottle of glistening retsina. "Two!" he followed the first with a second bottle setting them side by side so that the lustrous sheen of Aphrodite's lovely buttocks was reflected in the glass. He waved Matsoukas sternly to control himself. "And three!"

"Magnificent!" Matsoukas cried.

"We are not yet through," Cicero said. From his pocket he drew out a small thin metal box decorated with painted flowers.

"Schimmelpennincks!" Matsoukas released a long ardent sigh. He jumped toward the little dealer, who stood grinning at his pleasure, and hugged him in affection, taking care not to exert too much pressure on the small brittle frame. Then both men sprang quickly into action. Matsoukas drew a glittering corkscrew from the desk drawer. Cicero brought a pair of tumblers from the basin.

"Hurry, man!" the dealer said. "I am always three drinks behind the world and trying like hell to catch up!"

In a moment Matsoukas had deftly drawn the cork from the first bottle and filled each tumbler to the brim with wine. He raised his glass and sniffed the resiny aroma with his nostrils flaring.

"I drink to you, dear friend!" Matsoukas cried. "Your generosity, warmth, and soul are unequaled on this earth."

Cicero grinned and raised his own glass. "To the incomparable Matsoukas," he said. "A warrior poet with a spirit like a white-plumed helmet!"

By the first shadow of twilight they had finished the bread and the cheese, had emptied two bottles of wine, and were halfway through the last bottle. The wine had warmed them, relaxed their limbs, and swirled a meditative mist about their heads. Cicero was knotted like a pretzel in the chair behind the desk, while Matsoukas sprawled in one of the armchairs reserved for clients. He held his glass of wine in one hand, a delicate Schimmelpenninck in the other, contemplating the fine trail of smoke which rose from the ash.

"I tell you, old sport," Matsoukas said and he felt the words floating up his throat like bubbles to pop lightly at his lips, "there is only one way for eagles like us to survive. We must think like men of action and act like men of thought."

"That doesn't sound unreasonable," Cicero said, and his head wobbled slightly on his neck.

"I am against the machine," Matsoukas said. "The bloody machine has taken us from the land and bound us in these rotting cities."

"Right!" Cicero nodded with vigor and then reached up with a grimace to steady his head. "Can't even get a pack of smokes anymore without pushing the buttons on a damn vending machine."

Matsoukas somberly poured a fair measure of the remaining wine into his glass. Cicero stared with concern at the amount left in the bottle.

"I yearn often for the village festivals of Hellas," Matsoukas said. "The laughter of the girls running with their hair loose in the wind. The pitchers of cool wine when you come in hot and sweated from the fields." He paused sadly. "I tell you, dear friend, the city is a coffin where we no longer hear the nightingale's song."

Cicero raised his head and motioned Matsoukas gravely to silence. His lips pursed and he frowned in an effort to concentrate and then arched his arms and flapped them gently. "Whoop-ho!" he cried softly. "Whoop-hoop-hoop-hoop-ho!"

"What is that abominable sound?" Matsoukas asked sternly.

"A nightingale."

"Sounds more like a constipated hen," Matsoukas said reprovingly. "It is nothing we should jest about. We are living men, you and I, in a world of timid shadows."

Cicero studied the distance between his empty glass and the bottle.

"You have told me before," he said. "No flood, no hurricane, no fusillade of shot or shell can lay us low." He leaned forward in the chair to claim the last wine in the bottle perilously close to Matsoukas. "In the lines of your immortal poet," Cicero cried, "we are eagles soaring skyward!"

He had shifted his body too far and the swivel of the chair slipped on the broken bearing. The seat snapped forward like a catapult and with incredible swiftness Cicero was hurled off and disappeared under the desk.

Matsoukas stared in shock at the empty chair. Then he leaped up and ran around the desk. He bent down and tenderly raised the crumpled little dealer in his arms. He tried to stand him on his feet but Cicero's knees buckled and he would have fallen except for Matsoukas holding him. He struggled to regain his breath, his mouth opening and closing without uttering a sound.

"Are you all right, my friend?" Matsoukas cried. "Does anything feel broken?"

Cicero looked at Matsoukas with his ears quivering. Then he bent in what appeared to be a spasm of pain. His narrow shoulders trembled and he held his belly.

"Hold on, dear friend!" Matsoukas cried. "I will go for a doctor! Hold on!" He turned to leap for the door but Cicero managed to grab his arm. He saw tears in Cicero's eyes and a weird gurgling erupting at his lips.

"You are laughing!" Matsoukas said shocked. "You have gone mad!"

For a full minute Cicero continued to laugh wildly, his body wracked by fits of mirth, while Matsoukas watched him in dismay. When it seemed the dealer was finally about to compose himself, he caught sight of the swivel chair perched crookedly to the side and whirled off into another shrill spasm. Matsoukas led him to one of the armchairs and Cicero sat there holding his aching sides. He took a few deep draughts of breath.

"Hysteria," Matsoukas said consolingly. "The shock of the fall. Stay calm and it will pass."

"Matsoukas," Cicero said and paused and shook his head and whistled through his trembling lips. He looked at the chair behind the desk and began to shake again.

"Compose yourself, man!" Matsoukas cried. "What is so bloody funny?"

Slowly the little dealer grew calmer. He sat studying Matsoukas with a strange perceptive light in his eyes.

"Matsoukas," he said finally. "Matsoukas, do you know that if I were not your friend, I would not believe you or this place existed?"

"What do you mean?" Matsoukas asked with a shade of indignation.

Cicero drew out his handkerchief and slowly wiped his eyes and then blew his nose.

"Do you know why I love you, Matsoukas?" he said. "It is because in an absurd world you make absurd sense." He rose slowly and with a grimace tested one leg, bending the knee gingerly.

"Are you all right?" Matsoukas asked anxiously.

Cicero waved aside his concern. "I watch you, Matsoukas," he said. "I feel admiration and terror as well as love. I ask myself what will happen to you, what is your destiny?"

"Send a messenger to consult the oracle at Delphi," Matsoukas laughed.

"The old scourges were pestilence, the desert, and the wilderness," Cicero said. "Today they are fear, boredom, hopelessness, and despair. But you move serenely unmarked through them all. Your heels are run down, your cuffs shabby, your collar frayed, and yet you move with the vigor of a man born to set his situation right."

"Listen, old sport," Matsoukas said gently. "You have a plausible exterior and at the cardtable a prophetic soul, but at the moment you are unbalanced by shock and retsina."

"You have never learned to accept boundaries," Cicero said. "The boundaries in which human action and human judgment are enclosed. You give life the offering of an undivided heart."

"I am seriously concerned for you," Matsoukas said. "That was a nasty fall. I promise to fix that cursed chair."

Cicero moved a few steps weakly and braced himself against a corner of the desk. When Matsoukas started to aid him he waved him away.

"Stay where you are," he said with a wink. "I sway slightly like a ship riding low in the water but I do not sink. I have even survived your damn torpedo."

"You talk of mysteries," Matsoukas said. "The greatest mystery to me is what keeps you afloat when you are four-fifths submerged."

Cicero laughed and walked unsteadily to the window. He leaned his hands upon the sill, staring down for a moment into the darkness. When he turned to confront Matsoukas, a shadow crossed his thin pale face and his eyes seemed veiled suddenly in pools of darkness.

"Matsoukas," he said, and he released the word with a curious gentleness, "I will tell you what I think. You are a man chosen by the gods for eternal disaster, endless catastrophe. But you take every act of theirs prepared for your punishment, the blows they select to wound you, and you turn them into a kind of triumph...you are never defeated and you remain free. And how they must burn with anger and frenzy and how they must plot to bring you down." A glitter of fear scaled his cheeks. "It terrifies me to associate with you, to help you, to aid you. I love you, my friend, but you scare hell out of me." His voice gained a measure of strength. "Yet in this moment I give up my wretched neutrality. I am joining your battle. I cast my lot with you."

"Splendid!" Matsoukas cried. "Now that we have joined forces, we are an army!"

"I am not joking," Cicero said earnestly. "I am not fooling." He straightened his small narrow shoulders, holding his head erect, opening his eyes against the heavy-lidded tug of the wine. "I have twelve hundred dollars saved in the bank," he said gravely. "I want you to use this money to go with your son to Greece."

Matsoukas heard the words followed by a sudden roaring in his ears. For a moment they whirled off in a disordered wind and then they burned back across his body.

"You drunken twit!" he roared. "You joke about something like that! You bloody fool!"

Cicero watched him calmly. Matsoukas fell silent. A great wave of trembling swept his body. He realized slowly in the way Cicero looked at him, the way he waited, that the words had been sincere.

"Then you are mad!" Matsoukas said angrily. "Why should I take your savings for our journey? I have been saving for more than a year. I have a fair amount put aside. A good poker night or a solid parlay will send us aloft!"

"Listen to me, Matsoukas," Cicero said sternly. "If you are going to go at all, you must go now. Now! And the only way you can go now is on my money." He waved down Matsoukas furiously. "Will you let me finish? I tell you I have it planned. I have been considering it for months but I was frightened, unsure. Tonight when I took off like a rocket, it cleared my head. I don't need the damn money. I have been saving it and spending it for years. If anything happens to me one of my harpy sisters, the dragon in Kenosha, or the shark in Battle Creek will share it. I want you to have it on condition you prepare to leave at once. Get your son ready for the trip."

"Cicero, in the name of God," Matsoukas began.

"Will you let me finish?" Cicero cried. "Now listen. In the morning after I finish dealing I will meet you in the Olympia bar around 9:30. We will go to the bank together and draw out the money. Make your reservations and we will pick them up. I'll even go with you to the airport. I want to make sure nothing happens to you before you get on that bloody plane."

He moved suddenly toward the door, pulling down the sleeves of his shirt and coat.

"My friend . . ." Matsoukas said, and his voice wavered and a strange weakness flowed through his limbs.

"Yes, friend," Cicero said quietly. "And of all the things on this dark and unfathomable earth, I treasure your friendship most." With a final sardonic wink he left the office and closed the door. For an instant his spare frail body was outlined against the glass. Then he was gone and Matsoukas heard his steps receding down the stairs.

He sat without moving for a long time. The sharp and jagged edges of the office began to soften and dissolve. He let his face drop slowly against his cupped hands. He closed himself into the nest of his palms, alone with the quickened beating of his heart.

Home, he thought, home. Stavros and I are going home.

He rose to his feet and a great shout burst from his throat to pound against the walls. He could not bear to stand still and paced around the small office. He cried out again, a wild cry of exultation. As the echoes of his voice faded, Akragas answered with a wild banging against the radiator downstairs.

He roared in delight and stamped with scorn upon the floor. He circled the office again, and stopping before the window snapped the shade to the top. Above the roofs of the buildings the sky loomed dark and huge, the timeless curve of the night containing the flickering stations of the stars.

He saw his face reflected in the glass, the trunk of his body a solid mass. He raised his arms and held them out at his shoulders. They spanned the wide frame of the window like great wings trembling to spring aloft and cleave passage through the dark void of the night. For a moment he felt himself suspended on the precipice of the earth, full of incredible strength and vigor. Then he remembered his son. I will go and tell Stavros, he thought. I will go and prepare my son.

A movement in the alley below caught his eye. Anthoula had emerged from the kitchen of the bakery, her white frock glistening in the darkness, the square of light from the warm kitchen bathing her in a kind of mist.

He stood there knowing he was clearly outlined against the room behind him. Then she looked up. He could not see her face but he felt her eyes. He felt the quickened stirring of her breath. She turned and walked back inside. The door closed slowly. He saw her peering out, a sliver of light narrowing behind her, and then the darkness returned.

He felt suddenly a fierce desire to lay his hands upon her. His palms felt dry and he yearned to moisten them on the wild juices of her body.

He turned and started from the office. He knew in a great tearing fever that this was the night he would have her, make her feel the roaring of his love, this night, this matchless night, when he stood on the threshold of his dream.

CHAPTER EIGHT

Drizzle of rain upon the evening city. Across the street from the light-dimmed windows of the bakery, Matsoukas, shaken with assorted hungers, huddled in the doorway of a vacant store. The broken gutter above him released a stream of rain past his face. Through the cascade he impatiently watched old lady Barboonis wiping the empty glass showcases. He could almost hear the creaking of her rusty joints as she bent and stooped. Now and then, when a car passed and momentarily obscured his view, he closed his eyes and breathed the scent of a small sprig of violets he had bought from a street vendor.

He stood furiously impatient, afraid his mood of exultation might be dulled by waiting. The old lady disappeared into the kitchen. She returned carrying her coat. Matsoukas felt a tingle of anticipation careening through his tense body. She stood for what seemed an eternity struggling into her coat and waited, peering through the front door.

She is afraid her wretched prune-pit teats will melt, Matsoukas thought in despair. As he was about to groan she moved to flick off the last lights in the window. Only a small bulb still burned in the front of the shop, and the narrow doorway to the lighted kitchen in the back where Anthoula worked.

The old lady finally emerged from the shop, locking the door behind her. She hesitated with her head darting back and forth between sky and street like a petulant chicken. From her side she snapped up an umbrella and it burst into a black peaked shroud over her head. She disappeared beneath it and sped down the street with quick brittle steps.

When she turned the corner Matsoukas sprinted from the doorway. He darted across the street and passed the bakery going in the opposite direction from the old lady, his head bent into his collar, a sprinkle of rain whipping across his cheeks and ears. He walked rapidly up the alley to the back door of the bakery. He listened at the door and heard faint sounds of movement from within. He felt his flesh bunch in layers of excitement and he knocked softly on the frame of the door. When there was no answer, he knocked again, harder.

He heard her voice raised in inquiry and edged sharply with caution. He spoke with his lips pressed almost against the wood.

"It is Matsoukas," he said slowly.

There was silence from the kitchen.

"Matsoukas," he said more loudly. "Your neighbor, Matsoukas."

He waited for moments in a fretful disorder. He was about to knock and call out again when he heard the grating of a bolt snapped back and then a narrow strip of light tightly harnessed by a strong chain. The light blinded him and gave the visible portion of her white-clad body a strange luminosity.

"Forgive me," he said softly. "I did not mean to frighten you. I would like to talk to you."

"The store is closed," she said. "I am baking now." He sought in vain for a trace of warmth in her voice.

"I came to see you," he said.

She did not answer. He held himself stiffly, not wishing to make another move forward or even a motion to retreat until she had given him a sign. She closed the door and he groaned softly. Then he heard the spring of the chain and the door opened in a great burst of light.

He entered the dry hot scents of flour and yeast, the sweet aroma of walnuts and honey. He closed the door quickly behind him. She stood watching him, her hair bound up in coiled braids, the metal of comb and pins glistening within the dark waves. There were smudges of flour on her bare arms and a black currant glittered like a dark jewel at her throat. He was disconcerted by her eyes. He had never seen them as close before and there was a dark and enigmatic quality about them.

Before she could speak he mutely extended the sprig of flowers to her. The rain glistened on the purple petals and reflected the light of the kitchen with tips of flame. She stared at the flowers and then slowly looked back at him. A strange shaken distress was in her cheeks.

She did not reach for the flowers and he withdrew his hand. He walked toward a sink in the corner and picked a tall glass. He filled the glass with water from the tap and put in the violets. He set the glass on a small ledge. Then he turned and walked to a chair against the wall and sat down.

She had not moved but stood watching him. For an instant more they remained like that, she standing and he sitting, looking at one another. He felt the whole of the earth receding to leave them enclosed within a warm cocoon.

"Mr. Matsoukas . . ." she began slowly.

He cut her off with a quick wave of his hand.

"Matsoukas, please," he said. "Call me Matsoukas. All my friends do." He smiled. "Now please go on with your work. I will not disturb you."

She stared at him for another moment and then turned to the large pan of raised dough on the heavy center table. She bent slightly and assaulted the dough with a sudden burst of vigor, kneading it within her strong fingers.

In the beginning she worked stiffly, conscious of his presence, uneasy under his eyes. After a little while she caught the rhythm of the kneading and worked almost as if he were not there.

Matsoukas was massively moved by the splendor of the images she made burst into life. There was something of a shepherd's dance in the way she swayed, the sensual force of a peasant woman bending to draw water from a well. The light sweeping at intervals across her cheek and throat recalled for him the blinding circles of the moon across an open sea. He felt a raging in his blood.

"We live in a dark age," he said, and his voice trembled. "An age where men say one thing and mean another. A time of dwarfs afraid of life. A time of robots who cannot laugh or cry."

She made no sign that she heard. Her fingers pulled

116

and tugged at the dough. A dark strand of her hair fell loose across her cheek.

"I am not ashamed of what I am going to tell you now," he said. "I am a man bred of the Cretan earth and my emotions are violent. Let those who squeak of life feel shame. I feel no shame because for months I have watched you from my window, entered the bakery a hundred times to catch a glimpse of you, written numerous poems to you that I have destroyed. I feel no shame because I have come to love you."

She caught her breath. She paused, her hands buried to the wrist in the dough, and stared at him for a strange shaken moment. A pulse stirred in her throat and he felt himself swept by a quiver of tenderness.

"I love you, Anthoula," he said. "I have waited all these months to speak because I respected your grief. I have a wife, daughters, and a son. I have no right to speak. But I tell you now that I love you. And I feel no shame for that."

He thought then she was going to speak but she could not seem to find the words. She bent back to her work in distress. But a change had come over her. Her movements were sharp and driven, her arms taut, her fingers almost savage. She tugged at the dough with a kind of fury and defiance, seeking to subdue the thrust of her nipples against her blouse, the swell of her hips beneath the skirt of her shift. But her body trembled with a resurgence she could not control, a released ardor sweeping her limbs, washing the blunt edges of cold grief in a healing balm.

He watched in awe the immensity of her struggle. She walked from the table to the ovens, and on the walls her harried shadow rose and fell and like a frantic wraith would not be shaken loose.

And then suddenly as if she could endure it no longer, she turned to him. The stains of flour rose like foam at her wrists.

"Will you go now," she said and the words came from her lips in a distraught plea. "Will you please go now?"

"I do not want to go," he said quietly. "And I do not think you want me to go."

He was sorry for the pain of anguish upon her cheeks, an anguish evident in the way she stood and in her tumultuous silence.

"I am not the woman you seek, Matsoukas," she said. "You come in here and speak of love and I am not the woman you seek. I am not even beautiful."

"You are not beautiful?" he cried. "Listen to me! I cry out your dimensions. Here, I say, everyone listen. Anthoula is five feet six inches tall. Her waist is twenty-five inches, her bust and hips forty inches."

"These figures mean nothing."

"They are of immense significance to me," he said. "They define the space in which you move. Wherever you are this is the amount of space you require and this is the amount of space I will love."

"You speak easily of love," she said.

"Love unites us with all that is divine," he said.

She was silent for a moment and when she spoke, a cold weariness swept her cheeks.

"Is this then divine?" she asked. "The two of us poised like a ram and a sheep? You with a wife and family. I, with memories of my dead."

"There are laws of the heart," Matsoukas said, "which transcend the laws of men."

Her face across the table gleamed like a distant moon. "You do not know me," she said. "You do not really know who I am."

"I know you," he said softly. "I know you and my heart is clay waiting to be fired in the flame of your affection."

She stirred uneasily and brought her hands together, her fingers pulling helplessly at the cord of her shift.

"I live in darkness," she said. "Darkness is all around me."

"You cannot live in darkness," he said, "like a small hard fruit, rotting away, going into death with all your sweetness drying up. Your husband would not have wanted that."

"You did not know my husband," she said. "Many times he told me he would rather have me dead than in another man's arms."

"He could not know he would die," Matsoukas said.

"I think sometimes he died to make me his forever," she whispered. Her fingers rose and touched the chain at her throat. She pulled it slowly from the bodice of her dress. For the first time he saw the glittering gold ring suspended from the chain, a solid heavy band that was mate to the slimmer golden band on her finger. He stared at it uneasily.

"I am weary of life," she said, and shook her head in despair. "I pray that death will come to take me. I will go gladly and I will be at peace and my husband will rest as well."

"You must not talk like that!" Matsoukas cried and went to stand directly across the table from her. "Life is a chain and when people love the chain is strong. Defeat and despair are broken links. When enough links are broken, all the chain comes apart."

"I am talking of death," she said.

"Sorrow and fear are a kind of death too," he said.

"I know them well," she said.

He walked around the table and went to stand before her. There was a blossom of silence over the moment, a silence that concealed many things. He raised his hand to her cheek and felt her flesh cold beneath his fingers.

"Let me love you," he whispered. "Let me return you to love and to life."

She moved her cheek slightly and his fingers fell away.

"You must love," he said. "Love is in your long and shapely neck which carries your head with pride and grace. Love is in your mouth which turns down at the corners like the mouths of some of Michelangelo's women, mouths made to bite into a lover's lips. Love is in your body which is a bountiful orchard, a blending together of the rich juices and wild scents of numerous fruits, the orange and the lemon, the peach and the persimmon."

He saw the bonds of the past falling from her face, leaving her cheeks unfettered, her eyes reflecting him.

"You are even more than all that," he said. "You are like the scarlet thread woven into the white sails of old ships. You are a comfort and a solace. You are answer to the dark and dreadful lie that life is bondage, for to love you is to be free of loneliness and free from grief."

He knew she was listening more intently than she had ever listened to him before. Emboldened, he raised his hands again and placed them lightly about her arms, feeling her flesh tingle through his fingers. A vein throbbed against her throat, dark within the paleness of her flesh.

"Matsoukas," she said, and the name came in a strange and tearstained tenderness from her lips. He could never remember hearing his name spoken in that way before.

She reached up then to pull the cord of the center light. He saw the musky glitter of hair in her armpit and was filled with an ache of desire. The kitchen sprang into shadow and she stood outlined darkly under the single bulb from the small stairway that he knew led to her flat. He saw the glitter of her eyes, misted and shining, and realized that she was crying. She moved toward the stairs and walked up slowly. He followed closely behind her.

He waited, naked, between the sheets of her bed while she undressed and washed behind the closed bathroom door. He could hear the water running in the basin.

A pale wan glow of light fell from the parlor into the shadowed bedroom. In its shimmer he saw the room was a nest, warm and scented and cluttered. The walls were papered in patterns of coiled flowers. There were fragile-stemmed lamps adorned with shades of tear-shaped crystals. A large oval mirror glistened on the wall, a remnant of some baroque magnificence. At the foot of the bed were a dozen assorted pillows.

And the room contained as well that which was not visible but was there, a scent of powder and loneliness, a vapor born of all the nights she had lain alone, stirring fitfully in the futile embrace of memory.

He felt himself caught in a sweep of melancholia and

thought with a sudden resurgence of spirit of the journey. He was filled again with such jubilation that he could not bear to remain still. He threw back the sheet and walked on bare feet to the curtained window. He pulled the curtains apart slightly and peered out at the darkened window of his office across the way. Rain glistened against the glass. Something stirred at that window and he had the startled impression he was being watched. He drew back quickly and closed the curtains. After an instant he opened them warily again. He felt strangely disembodied, standing at both windows, occupying both rooms at the same time. For a confused second he was not sure where he really was. Then he sneered at the image of the familiar fool across the way.

"I am here," he said softly. "I am the one who is here. You are the shadow."

The water in the bathroom was turned off and he hurried back to the bed. He had just gotten beneath the sheet when the bathroom door opened. Anthoula emerged and she was wearing a long peignoir, her body outlined through its sheerness. She had taken down her hair and it hung in two long gleaming tusks over her shoulders. She moved once more into shadow and then she was at the bed. She sat down on the edge and he moved from beneath the sheet and put his hands on her shoulders and drew her slowly down beside him.

Her head hung back against the sheet and the skin of her face gleamed with a dreadful whiteness as if all her blood had drained away. His fingertips moved along her nape and into the great soft coils of her hair. He reached down through the strands and embraced her breasts, pulling aside the silk of the robe so they sprang free, large juice-heavy fruit with nipples chilled like buds denied the sun. He bent then and gravely kissed each nipple in consolation. He twisted then to find her mouth, rolled hard upon her, and with his chest leveled the firm high slopes of her breasts. Something cold and hard cut against his flesh, something he felt like the tip of an unsheathed knife.

He sprang back from her body and knelt trembling with the chill of the touch. He peered closer and around her throat, esconced on the chain, he saw the dead husband's ring glittering with an eerie light.

He moved upon her again but however he sought to embrace her, the chain with the ring was there. It lay between her breasts, flowing toward him with each crest of her breath. And before it the hard thrust of his desire wavered and a worm of weakness shattered his core.

Finally, hung with failure and futility, he caught his fingers angrily in the chain, closed tightly upon it. He wanted to tear it off although he knew it would cut her flesh. He began to pull, slowly at first and then with mounting urgency, hoping the clasp would break. When she sensed what he was doing he was not prepared for her frenzy.

She cried out from some hidden core of her being, a terrible cry of betrayal and fear. She raised her hands to her throat to protect the ring. When she could not withstand his strength she let go the chain and with her fingers bent in the shapes of claws flew at his face. He felt her nails like the talons of a wild bird claw at the flesh of his cheek. He cried out then and released the chain.

For a few dreadful moments they lay like that, naked

and divided, and he plotted furiously the way to assault her again. He felt her stiffen beside him, a cold fear radiating from her body.

"Holy Jesus," she said, and her voice was shredded with terror. "O Holy Jesus."

"What is wrong?" he cried, and pain and despair added fire to his words. In that instant he was conscious of another presence within the room.

He leaped from the bed to crouch naked, his muscled arms extended in a wrestler's stance, waving a challenge toward the shadows in the corners. He sensed the presence behind him, whirled around, and could see nothing. Yet something was in the room, something neither animal or human, a malignant and mocking wraith capering about their heads.

"Who are you?" Matsoukas cried. "What do you want?"

Even as he watched with the hair of his testicles bristling, the wraith simulated every gesture of some savage dance, leaps, spins, somersaults, backbends, all to the tuneless scream of some wild music.

He turned back to Anthoula, snatching at her flesh with a frenzy of his own, assaulting her nipples and her loins. In terror of the demon she fought back fiercely, while around their heads the desiccated tail lashed like a whip, and the discordance of bells, rattles, and bull bladders beat against their ears.

He would not release her, knowing if he did that she would be forever lost. Against this condemnation he performed with a rampant artifice and guile. He fought a dazzling dance on her body, toe-touchings, beats, turns, twists, arms raised, legs together and apart, back humped and swayed, hand grasps, arm hooks, and cross grasps.

The battle rose to a fevered pitch and in desperation he swept her up, spun her over, her breasts mashed against the sheet, imprisoning the ring, her buttocks hung before him. For a moment their bodies poised suspended on the precipice of the earth, then, holding her thighs like the frame of a chariot, he drove forward and down.

He roweled the mares with a shout and lashed forward and away. He heard the stamp of cloven feet behind him and he drove with abandon and fury, pulling on the right and then the left, meeting each maddened lunge of the steeds with a firm rooted stance of his own.

Rocks sailed about them, struck sparks from their wheels, the black and lustrous wings of birds beat about their ears, thin columns of smoke rose in the shadows. They hurtled toward the rock-bound shore of a somber sea, dead of any flower but mosses, seaweed and shell along the desolate bays. He felt the salt-flakes on his chest and the mares became brutal dolphins plunging beneath the dark surface of the storm-ravaged waters, above the whitened and sepulchred hulls of sunken ships.

They sprang from the sea in a great wave of spray and above them glittered the fiery purple dawn. They surged up a turret-circled steep of cloud, across the spangled arc of the sky, into a landscape of bloodstained sun.

A searing cry ripped the heavens. The cry faded, haunting as the echoes of a lute. The earth returned in a sonorous calm. He fell across her quivering legs and like a great beached whale, flopped on his side.

Anthoula's face was close to him, her eyes filled with a massive wonder and warmth. She moved slightly to draw closer to his body and put the palm of her hand upon his flesh, stroking the dark curled tangle of hair on his chest with awe and ardency. Even as her fingers tickled and he started to howl with laughter, he thought again of the coming journey, Stavros and he taking flight, and the laughter became a great hoarse and triumphant cry.

CHAPTER NINE

HE entered the spacious splendor of the airline ticket office downtown and stood for
a moment inside the door. He marveled at
the opulence and beauty of the surroundings, the carpeted
and paneled magnificence of the high-ceilinged and venerable enclosure. It might have been the throne room of
some king's palace.

His attention was swept to a massive map of the world
adorning one full wall, a map showing continents and
oceans crisscrossed by an assembly of sharp red lines.
These traced the routes the airline flew. He approached
the wall and under his breath with poignant delight he
read off the names of the capitals. Paris . . . Geneva . . .
Rome . . . and then, Athens. His gaze lingered on that
flower of cities marked by a single glittering pin. From
there the distance to his beloved Crete could be measured
with the tip of his finger.

He turned under a surge of excitement and moved
briskly toward the long counter where a half-dozen trim
and chic young women waited eagerly to serve him. He
approached one lovely and short-haired girl with a be-
guiling smile.

"Athens!" he said loudly to her. He swept his hand in

a majestic gesture toward the great map. "Two tickets for Athens, Greece!" He was rewarded by several of the other young women looking his way with what he understood to be admiration. "One ticket for myself and one ticket for my son who is seven."

She made a rapid notation on a pad. "Yes sir," she said brightly. "When would you like to go?"

He looked at her and nodded gravely. The question was the most pertinent one and he appreciated her asking it at once. "As soon as possible," he said. "Even sooner."

She picked up a timetable and leafed through it with admirable efficiency. "Our next flight for Athens is tomorrow morning, Saturday," she said. "I can check if there are two seats available."

"Splendid!" he said. With a shade of impatience he remembered the young Cournos boy he had promised a wrestling lesson in the morning at the gym. For an instant he considered taking the flight anyway and then he shook his head. "I have a business appointment tomorrow morning," he said regretfully.

"The next flight will be early Sunday morning," she said.

"That will be fine," he said.

She made another notation on her pad. He was delighted at how smoothly everything was proceeding.

"First class or economy?"

"Economy."

"Round trip?"

"One way," he said.

"Do you have your passport?"

He drew it from his pocket and handed it to her with a flourish.

"Leonidas Matsoukas and son Stavros," he said.

She nodded as she examined it and copied the names down on her pad.

"You will need smallpox inoculations," she said.

"I roused the doctor at dawn this morning," he said gleefully. "My son and I both received our shots."

She smiled and picked up the phone. He listened with jubilation as she confirmed his reservation. She hung up the phone and drew out a blank ticket. He leaned forward slightly and watched her filling in their names and the flight.

"Your flight number 227 will leave at 5:00 A.M. Sunday morning," she said, "arriving in New York at 8:10 A.M. You leave New York at 9:15 A.M. and after a single stop in Rome arrive in Athens after a total flight time of eight and a half hours."

"Marvelous!" he said. He was astonished at how easily the whole transaction had been accomplished.

"That will be seven hundred and forty dollars," she said.

"Right!" he said seriously. "Please hold the tickets right here. I am going at this moment to meet my business associate." He coughed discreetly. "He is liquidating some investments for me and we will return with the cash."

She smiled once more and put down her pen. "We will hold them right at the will-call counter, Mr. Matsoukas."

"What time do you close?" he asked.

"At nine this evening."

"I will be here hours before that," he said. He moved away from the counter and then turned anxiously back. "If you have to leave, Miss, will you be sure to have the tickets here with someone else?"

"They will be held here under your name," she said.

Back in the neighborhood after a bus ride from downtown, he spent thirty minutes appraising luggage in the pawnshop of Oboleski.

"That is a sturdy bag, Matsoukas," Oboleski said. "Hardly used at all."

"Save those lies for your other poor customers," Matsoukas said sharply. "The straps are weak and the bottom is stitched together with glue. I have told you, lout, that this bag is for no short lazy trip across a lake. We are crossing the world."

His gaze caught on a stout leather bag on a shelf in back of the counter. "That one," he pointed. "That one is a treasure. I can see the quality from here."

Oboleski threw up his hands in admiration. "You have the eyes of a hawk, Matsoukas," he said. "That is one of the best bags I have in the store. A wealthy young man from Evanston pawned it because it belonged to his father who passed away. The boy couldn't bear to be reminded of the beloved old man."

"Hide the bloody case history," Matsoukas said. "How much?"

Oboleski looked at him in apprehension. "Ten dollars," he said in a low voice.

Matsoukas did not disappoint him. "Robber!" Matsoukas cried. "Thief! Let me see the entry. If you gave that poor devil more than two dollars, I will eat the book!"

"Overhead, Matsoukas," Oboleski pleaded.

"Four dollars," Matsoukas said. "That will take care of overhead and all."

"Five dollars," Oboleski said. "Because I value your friendship."

"You are a dense-souled scoundrel and do not give a damn about my friendship," Matsoukas said. "Four-fifty and not a cent more."

"Cash?"

"Of course," Matsoukas said impatiently.

Oboleski sighed. "Four-fifty then," he said. He stared sharply at Matsoukas. "You do have four-fifty?"

"O weasel of little faith," Matsoukas said scornfully. "I have just purchased tickets for Greece at a cost of more than a thousand dollars."

Oboleski sniffed. "Do you have four-fifty left?"

"I will be back in several hours," Matsoukas said. "I will have the money then."

Oboleski groaned. He picked up the bag and carried it dolefully behind the counter to place it back on the shelf.

"I will return!" Matsoukas cried. "Sell that bag and I will suspend you by your callous-riddled feet from the globes outside!"

Sitting on a stool at the Olympia bar, Matsoukas waved his glass of ouzo cheerfully at the bartender, Toundas, nervously wiping glasses behind the bar.

"I will see them all again," Matsoukas said. "The River Nestos, and the Cathedral in Rhodes. The island fort of Bourtzi on Nauplia, and the tragic bridge of Arta. I will see all those blessed places again."

"Wonderful," Toundas licked his lips. "That will be thirty cents for the ouzo, Matsoukas," he smiled weakly.

"There is no sight on this earth more serene than a shepherd at twilight," Matsoukas said, "leading his flock to the grazing grounds."

"Lovely," Toundas tried to speak heartily. His lips twisted. "Can you pay me now, Matsoukas?" he asked plaintively. "I may get busy and forget to collect."

"And I will dance again in Crete to the three-stringed lyre," Matsoukas said. "I tell you, old sport, to dance to a Cretan lyre is to invade the domain of the Gods."

"I will do some dancing myself tonight if the boss finds the drawer short thirty cents," Toundas tried to laugh but managed only a mirthless squeak.

Matsoukas turned to look at the clock on the wall which read twenty minutes past ten. "Cicero is late," he said. He sighed. "The blessed man probably fell asleep at the Minoan. I will speed over there and rouse him." He slipped swiftly off the stool. "If he comes in meanwhile, ask him to go over to my office and wait for me." He started for the door. "See you later, old sport."

"I may not be here," Toundas called grievously after him. "I may be looking for another job."

He tried the front door of the Minoan Music Store even though he knew that Falconis did not open until noon. He walked around to the alley door that was tightly barred. He knocked several times on the chance that Cicero was still inside, asleep.

He walked impatiently to the building where Cicero lived, ascended the stairs to the dealer's room and knocked on his door. He knocked again more loudly and then bent and peered through the keyhole. He could only see the foot of the bed, disheveled as usual, not revealing whether the bed was occupied or not. He knocked again, waited another moment, and then pulled an envelope from his pocket. He scrawled a note on the back that he would be waiting for Cicero in his office. He slipped the envelope under the door.

On the way back to his office he detoured a block to the Midtown Bank where he knew Cicero had his account. He walked briskly in through the revolving door and stood for a moment in the vaulted and colonnaded interior. From all the cages rose the sibilant murmur of money passing back and forth. He circled the bank checking the lines at each window for Cicero. All the time he breathed deeply the effervescent scents of cash. It gave him an emollient feeling of delight, producing the same pleasing little ripples of gas that a hearty meal with a bottle of wine achieved. He passed a fair wave of wind and smiled benignly at the uniformed guard who looked at him sharply.

He left the bank and walked rapidly to his office. He paused in the grocery downstairs where Akragas was short-weighting clusters of grapes.

"Has my friend, Cicero, been in looking for me?"

The grocer sneered and did not answer. Matsoukas waited in an ominous silence. The grocer finally mumbled no.

Matsoukas started for the stairs. "I will be vacating these abominable premises effective tomorrow," he called back over his shoulder. "I am going to Greece."

Akragas waited until he had reached the top of the stairs. "More likely you will go to jail!" he hollered.

In his office Matsoukas paced around his desk. He appraised his belongings and felt a pang of regret at leaving them behind. He would have to bring in a stout wooden crate and wrap his treasures carefully for storage.

He sat down at his desk. He made a note to be sure to take his wrestling belt on the trip. He pulled the jar containing the Cretan earth to him. He uncapped it and poured some of the black earth into his palm. He felt it curl and throb against his flesh as if it contained some vibrant seed.

He felt in that moment a longing for the old country so intense that it surpassed any hunger he had ever known, any thirst, any love. He imagined himself ascending a path up the side of a white-capped mountain, Stavros secure in his arms. The sky above the peak would be luminous and blue, and clusters of blossom would flame on the shrubs and vines. Stretched out below them would be the cubed roofs of houses, the whitewashed taverns along the shore, and the sea, the blue-hued water glittering and clear, the ocean floor visible through fathomless depths. And even at twilight, he recalled now with awe, the sun would not sink into the sea. There was always another shadowy island to absorb it, another island between the sunset and the horizon, another sanctuary keeping the sun eternal.

He felt his breath grow short and his heart beginning to pound. He could not bear to remain still and after pouring the black earth back into the jar he rose and descended the stairs.

"Tell Cicero to wait for me," he told Akragas.

"I am not an answering service," the grocer squawked.

"Listen, rump-head," Matsoukas said quietly. "Give him my message or you will not be able to speak at all."

He started from the grocery and crossed the street on his way back to Cicero's room and to wait for the Minoan to open. He passed the bakery at a vigorous clip as Anthoula was reaching into the window for a small tray of baklava. She saw him at the same instant he noticed her and the flame in her cheeks and eyes singed him through the glass. With a barely perceptible nod of her head, a flurried movement of her eyes, she bade him come around to the alley door.

He was anxious to reach Cicero but he did not wish to affront her. In addition even though less than twelve hours had passed since their first fierce union he recalled the feel of her body with a sharp tingling ardor in his flesh. He consoled himself that an hour more or less would do no harm.

He walked casually around the corner and started down the alley. He looked to make sure there was nobody watching and then slipped over to wait outside the bakery door. He heard the bolt snapped back on the other side. Anthoula opened the door and reached out and pulled him in. She embraced him with a silent but ardently weighted kiss that quivered his toenails and then motioned him up the stairs. He leaped swiftly on his toes for the stairway leading to her apartment. As he ascended the stairs with muffled treads he heard her speaking to the old lady in the front of the store.

"I have a headache," Anthoula spoke in a grieving voice. "I am going to sleep for an hour. Please do not disturb me."

Matsoukas waited at the top of the landing and watched her sweep like a wild wraith up the stairs, her apron whipping the walls, until with a kind of frenzy, she exploded into his arms.

Later, when she moved from the bed, for the first time in daylight he saw the full blossom of her nakedness. From his angle of vision she loomed above him in terraces of beauty. She bent once to kiss his shoulder where she had bitten him in passion, and her breasts, full and tipped with daggered nipples, stabbed against his arm.

"My darling," she whispered. "O my darling."

She raised the filmy peignoir and slipped her arms lazily into the sleeves. She let it hang open dividing her breasts by twin wisps of silk. She walked to the dressing table and sat down. She stared back to where he lay naked in the bed, sheet across his belly, his arms raised and folded under his head. She blew him a kiss.

"I adore you," she said.

She raised her arms and pulled loose the length of her hair until it hung like a ruffled cape almost to her waist. She bent her head forward and then to one side so that the great abundance of hair tumbled into thick sections. She picked up a boar-bristled brush from the vanity table and went at each tusk, brushing with long vigorous strokes.

He watched with wonder at the way each thrust caused her hair to rise and quiver, growing fuller and shaking off glitters of light. Finally, when she arched her head back, her hair had become enormous, radiating like a sunburst about her temples and cheeks.

"You are a vision," he said softly.

He remembered Cicero and sneaked a quick look at his watch. He had been with Anthoula almost an hour and he made an effort to rise but his body felt drained. He marveled again at the intensity of her passion. Impaled within her he had felt her closing on him as if her body were a great claw seeking to pull him into her completely, capable of gorging all his blood and muscle and bone.

She saw him watching her and must have sensed what he was thinking for she laughed, a sensual vigorous laugh of fulfillment.

"You naughty boy," she said. "O you naughty boy."

She stuck out her long crimson tongue at him and then twisting toward him, the peignoir falling away from her breasts, she swiftly swept her hair up into the shape of a heart. With the mastery of a deft mimic she reshaped the mass into a sleek mound and tucked the backs under her fingers. She released the fall of hair again and pulled the strands away from her head in the shape of a butterfly's wings. Each new forming of hair changed her incredibly, and Matsoukas was astounded at how it transformed and altered the features of her face and the contours of her body. He realized he was witnessing some strange ritual of feminine sorcery, the ways in which a woman revealed to some hapless man another facet of her multifarious being.

He made another anxious effort to rise and she cried out hoarsely in protest and came sweeping back to the bed.

"I must go," he said quickly. "An important business appointment."

"Not yet!" she cried. She let the peignoir fall and moved upon him with a relentless nakedness. As he braced to meet her, he thought, is the woman a bottomless pit? Then remembering her long months of desolate abstinence he tightened in remorse and met her hunger with a surging violence of his own.

When he finally slipped from the kitchen door of the bakery, it was a little past noon. He was weary and exhausted, his body a mass of protesting flesh, his blood numbed by the fury of the rivets he had pounded. He hurried to the grocery across the alley.

"Is he upstairs?" he asked Akragas.

"Who?" the grocer sneered.

"Don't jest with me, cockroach!" Matsoukas cried. "Is my friend upstairs? Has he been here at all?"

The grocer blinked in fear and shook his head.

Matsoukas hurried through the streets to the Minoan Music Store. An edge of apprehension sliced at his flesh and he cursed the delay in Anthoula's bed.

The small bell above the door tinkled as he entered the Minoan and he swept under the archways and around the shelves to confront Falconis sitting at his desk. Matsoukas spoke against the tight fear growing in his body.

"Where is Cicero?" he asked.

Falconis was paler than usual and he looked at Matsoukas without answering.

"Man, where is Cicero!" Matsoukas cried.

Falconis watched him for a trembling moment more. His tongue came out to lick his dry lips.

"Last night while dealing," he said and he shivered, "he had a stroke."

Matsoukas heard the words and for a whirling instant they caused a roaring in his ears. He felt them echo and reecho through the span of his body cutting to the core of his being.

"We called the Mercy Hospital right away," Falconis said. "They sent an ambulance for him."

Matsoukas turned and, with the fear burst like a wound in his flesh, he ran toward the door.

"It wasn't my fault, Matsoukas," Falconis called plaintively after him. "I was always decent to . . ."

The slamming door cut off his words. Matsoukas stood for a frenzied moment undecided how to get to the hospital most quickly. A car was approaching and he leaped into its path and waved it down with a great swinging of his arms. The brakes squealed and the startled driver gaped at him through the windshield. Matsoukas ran around and entered the other door.

"Emergency," Matsoukas said. "Mercy Hospital a mile from here. Left at the next light."

The man looked at him a moment longer and then something in the frozen set of Matsoukas' cheeks and head started him driving.

The receptionist in the hospital lobby leafed through a file of cards, extracted one and studied it.

"We have notified his sisters," she said. "Are you a relative."

"A friend," Matsoukas said.

He carried the card to the elevator. A nurse at the fourth-floor desk took his card and motioned him to follow her. They moved down the corridor and he caught vagrant glimpses of occupied beds, still bodies, watchful and grieving faces. The nurse paused before a room at the end of the corridor and Matsoukas heard the wild rushing sound of wind.

He entered the room with dread and traced the wind from a small weird tent covering the upper part of Cicero's body, a hose running to a cylinder beside the bed. Below the perimeter of the tent Cicero's legs lay stiff and straight beneath the spread, seeming the slim thighs and calves of a child, the toes a wide distance from the bottom of the bed.

Matsoukas bent slightly to peer into the tent. He saw his friend's face luminated through the glass, the cheeks green and rippled as though they lay just beneath the scummed surface of a stagnant pool, the mouth gleaming like a shell, the moist hair plastered in tendrils of weed across his temples.

"Cicero, it is me," Matsoukas whispered. He saw the spasms of blood and phlegm bubbling in the hollows of Cicero's throat. And he sensed a stirring under the flesh and bone, the eyelids quivering in a massive effort to open.

"It is Matsoukas!" he cried softly. He reached down and caught the dealer's hand that lay just outside the tent. He felt a rawness to the flesh, a suspension between warmth and cold, a hard tautness to the wrist. He pressed the fingers in the enfolding shelter of his palm. And he was possessed by a frenzy to tear off the tent and embrace his friend.

"Cicero!" he pleaded. "Cicero!"

A harsh new sound made him tense. A strange knock ing that he heard clearly. It was a sound that he remem· bered suddenly from his childhood, he had thought it a bough striking against the house on the night his grandmother died. He had heard it while he lay in bed and it struck terror into his body. Now he heard the sound again and understood what it meant. He saw that darkness hung on the borders of the room, pressing in upon them with unwinding plumes of shadow. The light declined. All forms and shapes absorbed the relentless dark. And a wretched resignation burned his flesh.

For a long time he sat beside the bed holding Cicero's hand. Once the nurse entered silently and adjusted the knob on the tank and looked in through the glass. He rose a number of times and peered into the tent. His friend's face was more remote each time, blurred and fading, settling deeper into the water. In the end all that remained was a frail shell beneath a fathom of dark water, a tiny ripple left by the final mocking and tender quiver from his lips.

After a while, he could not be sure how long, he was conscious of a difference in the timbre of the wind, the disordered hiss of air rushing into a vacuum. He felt the long lean fingers grown cold and strangely still in his palm. He raised them to his lips and kissed them gently for the last time.

He walked to the tank and turned off the air. A total silence covered the room. He walked from there down the corridor to the small coned enclosure of light where the nurse sat. "He is dead," he told her. He pushed open the door marked with the red-lamped exit and started down the stairs.

Outside the evening had come, the pavements almost deserted in the hour of supper. He walked along the street, past a row of stores just closing, and entered the mouth of an alley.

He leaned against the brick of a wall and looked up at the curve of the sky. He felt the distant stars draw into the blurred circle of his grief. A lament curled in his ears, an ancient dirge, a wail carried over the centuries through dreams, by the wind through the peaks of trees, and by chilled stirrings in the blood.

He began walking deeper into the blackness of the alley. He started to moan softly, his flesh bunching and heaving in great cold shudders. Yet in his terrible anguish he could not understand whether he grieved for his friend or for his son.

CHAPTER TEN

MATSOUKAS sitting at his desk staring at the partially packed crate containing his possessions. Each morning when he entered his office he carefully wrapped in tissue and brown paper one more picture or statue or framed testimonial letter and placed them in the crate between cushions of crumpled newspaper.

Since the death of Cicero two weeks before he had added only about a dozen items to the crate. He would examine each article intently, wavering between what to take and what to leave behind. But in this way, the open crate before him, he remained suspended for the journey.

An occasional client entered for some advice and assistance. Matsoukas listened to the tales of woe and earnestly sought to aid them. But for the first time in years his attention drifted relentlessly away. He wondered how his bets were faring and he chafed with impatience for the client to leave so he might hurry downstairs and use the phone in the hallway to call Falconis.

"Listen, Matsoukas," Falconis told him fretfully, "this is the third call about this race. You know post time is not for another five minutes yet. I have never known you to be this unbalanced with impatience."

He had six times in the past two weeks altered his airline reservations. Having come so close to the journey he could not bear to be without seats on each flight that left for Greece. As his tickets were cancelled when he did not pick them up before the flight, he made another reservation.

He had attempted to obtain some special dispensation from the airlines, visiting their offices, sweeping whoever he was allowed to see with eloquent arguments why he should be charged only a single fare. He promised to hold Stavros tightly in his arms and not let him intrude by even an inch upon the seat beside them. All his passion was useless against the impersonal ritual of their response.

"Hello, Falconis!" he cried into the phone. "What did Araby do in the second?"

He listened to the answer and sighed. He rapidly consulted the scratch sheet he held in his hand.

"Give me five to win on Saragosa in the third ..." He heard the uneasy whine of Falconis cut into his words. "I will pay you, man!" he cried. "Have I not always paid in the end? These bets are important to me now!" Falconis succumbed with a doleful grunt. "All right, old sport," Matsoukas pressed his advantage, "and then parlay Saragosa with Valhalla in the fourth at Tropical for five more." He hung up quickly to avoid hearing Falconis squawk.

Once again at his desk he studied the pad containing the names of those he approached for a loan. One by one he had to scratch them off.

"I am sorry, Matsoukas," Fatsas told him sadly. "Forty years I have been playing cards. I do not have a dime and slim prospect of ever getting any more than a small stake to join another game."

"Can't help you, Matsoukas," Charilaos said glumly. "My guitar is in hock and without my guitar I cannot work to earn the money to redeem it."

"My wife is having a baby."

"I am getting a divorce."

"I am broke."

"You must be mad," Falconis told him. "You owe me almost six hundred dollars. Now you want me to lend you six hundred dollars more for you to leave the country so that I may never see either amount again."

"Listen, old sport," Matsoukas spoke earnestly. "I will find some work in Greece. I will send you every last dollar with any interest payment you wish. I need this money now."

Once or twice it seemed to him that Falconis wavered. But the bookie's fear of being thought weak made him freeze at an act so patently absurd.

Matsoukas remained in his office late at night concocting bold schemes to raise the cash for the fare. There were wild real estate projects, and an efficiency plan for restaurants in which a squad of chefs were rushed by limousine and driver to various restaurant kitchens. In this way a half-dozen places could be serviced with a sharing of the salaries. These ideas expired like seeds denied sun and water.

Of all his plans and designs, none excited him and nourished his hopes more than the master project he labeled, "Heavenly Burials." This project was born one night when walking the streets restlessly he paused before a cinema showing a film about a cemetery called "Whispering Glades." He stared for a long while at the sidewalk trailer photos of crematorium urns and flowered plots and a great glistening rocket. He hurried home and all the remainder of that night he worked out the details for the plan, possessed by exultation. At dawn he called the Archdiocese in an effort to obtain an audience with the Bishop. He called unsuccessfully several more times that day and the following day as well. All he was able to achieve was an appointment on the morning of the third day with a young Deacon on the Bishop's staff, a pale-faced and bespectacled youth only six months out of the seminary with a small sparse beard that was a pallid copy of the Bishop's thick and handsome tuft. The Deacon met Matsoukas at a bench in a corridor of the Archdiocese.

"Please sit down, Mr. Matsoukas," he spoke in a thin nervous voice. "This is a frantic morning. His Eminence is receiving many visitors of international importance and I am needed. But he has empowered me to listen carefully to your plan and relay the information to him for whatever further disposition might be required."

"I would have honestly preferred to have explained directly to his Eminence," Matsoukas said. "A plan of this magnitude requires contact at the highest possible level. If I had carried it to the Episcopalians I am positive I would have been granted audience with at least an Archbishop. But I could only consider offering it to our own beloved church."

The Deacon shifted his black-cassocked figure restlessly on the bench and cleared his throat. He stared somberly at Matsoukas through his heavy-lensed glasses. "We appreciate your loyalty and devotion," he said smoothly. "I will make sure that his Eminence hears of it should he wish to offer you his benevolent blessing."

"Which I will accept gratefully," Matsoukas said. He

drew a deep breath and looked carefully up and down the long corridor. "This project must be shrouded in the utmost secrecy," he said in a low voice. "If word of it leaked out, the Catholics might get a massive jump on us. It would be a catastrophe."

The Deacon leaned forward slightly. A flush of excitement speared his pale cheeks. "Go on," he said. "Please go on."

"Right!" Matsoukas said. "Now this is how we begin. We announce from the pulpit of every Greek Orthodox church in the diocese that an organization under the auspices of the Bishop himself will undertake funeral and special interment for a sum of five hundred dollars. This is one third the cost of the average funeral and we will handle every detail. From the moment a beloved member of the family dies we take charge. When we have signed a thousand agreements we will have a half-million dollars." He paused to let the size of the amount impress the Deacon. "Of course this amount may vary slightly since I am considering a twenty percent ecclesiastical discount for priests and their families..." And he added quickly, "... for Deacons too."

The Deacon blinked. "That seems fair," he said slowly. He looked slightly perplexed.

"Now," Matsoukas said, "as we receive the corpses of the first thousand who die, we cremate them..."

"Mr. Matsoukas!" the Deacon said in a shocked voice. "Are you acquainted with the position of our church on cremation? We are unalterably opposed..."

"Permit me to finish, your Deaconship," Matsoukas said brusquely. "This plan is so brilliant it may require that certain church codes be relaxed. Please listen carefully. At the same time that we are cremating the thousand corpses, we obtain a small surplus rocket from the United States Government. We enclose the ashes of the thousand heavenly pioneers into a special urn in the rocket and ..." he paused with tremors of excitement singeing his tongue ... "we launch the rocket with the ashes into space to become a satellite, whirling forever around the earth in God's pasture for a truly celestial interment!"

The Deacon staggered on the bench as if he had been kicked. He stared at Matsoukas in shock and tried to speak but only managed a weak squeak.

"Stuns you, doesn't it?" Matsoukas cried. "Takes your breath away! I knew you would be affected this way! But there is more to come. We launch this rocket in a mass blast-off ceremony at dawn from Soldier's Field or Yankee Stadium! Can you imagine the sight? The grandstand packed with tens of thousands of relatives and close friends of the deceased, watching them actually begin their final journey not into the damp and worm-riddled earth but to the stars! The Archbishop will be there, of course, and all the Bishops clad in their bright vestments and a choir of a thousand voices, one for each deceased, will thunder out a majestic chorus of hosanna, hosanna, hosanna!"

"My God!" the Deacon found his voice. "O my God!"

"Magnificent, isn't it?" Matsoukas cried gleefully. "The Presbyterians and Baptists will be green with envy and the Pope will burn a cluster of red hats! Instantly they will strive to imitate us but to no avail! The Orthodox Church will gain the envy and applause of the entire world! We will gain millions of new converts! Do you understand the significance? We will be the first faith into space!"

The Deacon struggled to rise and his legs would not sustain him. When he finally got to his feet he leaned weakly against the wall for support. He stared down at Matsoukas with his face as white as gravestone.

"My God!" he gasped again. "O my God!"

"God will be delighted, of course," Matsoukas said briskly, "but let us begin with the Bishop? Do you think I might see him now?"

The Deacon quivered and his thin crimson tongue came out to lick helplessly at his lips. Then he reached down and caught the hem of his cassock. He raised it to his knees and crouching slightly he started walking down the corridor with short quick steps.

"What is wrong?" Matsoukas rose and cried after him. "Just a minute, your Deaconship! You have not heard about the memorial service once a year! Wait!"

The Deacon looked back and then turned forward and hoisted his cassock higher and broke into a disjointed run. Holding the black cloth bunched at his thighs, he fled through the door at the end of the corridor.

When Matsoukas grew restless and uneasy he went to spend several hours with Anthoula. Whether it was day or night they bounced on her rocking bed. He was grateful for her long shrill shrieks of passion which smothered his distress and, for a little while, provided his agitation a rampant release. She never seemed to get enough of him and yet he always left her bed feeling he had stayed too long. His body ached and throbbed and he felt like a blacksmith engaged in an endless battle to shoe a wild and unbroken mare.

On other afternoons when a strange melancholy possessed him, he escaped from the frenzied milling crowd in the Minoan, and avoided Anthoula. He boarded a bus and rode to the end of the line, to the cemetery where Cicero had been buried. He walked beneath the metal arch of the gate along a gravel road. When he turned off the road he moved across a small hill, carefully wending his way between the monuments and markers. He came to Cicero's grave, the earth dark and loose and still unsettled. He squatted down beside the grave.

"How are you today, old sport?" he asked. He picked up a handful of earth, held it tightly in his palm for a moment and then let it slip through his fingers. "The boys at Falconis miss you," he said. "Fatsas plays even worse than his usual terrible game and Babalaros is even more impatient. Old Kampana senses you are absent and sniffs the air with disdain when another dealer calls the cards." He fell silent under a sudden tug of despair. "And I miss you too," he said.

A soft wind rippled the branches of the nearby trees and carried the whirling scents of spring to his nostrils. He was much more conscious here than he had been in the city that spring had erupted into bloom. The buds were longer and greener on the branches of the trees, and the birds were everywhere, speckled robins and gray starlings and brownish redwings.

"Are you getting acquainted here?" he asked. "Have you been introduced to the solid burghers and their somber wives? Is there among them a black sheep or two to keep you company?" He laughed wryly. "I cannot imagine you lying still, old sport, listening to the wind among the stones. The rest of your scrawny frame might be content to sleep but not your lovely fingers, your marvelous hands. I would give ten to one that even now when twilight falls they rise and roam among the graves flexing a deck of cards and trying to assemble a table of players for some stud."

He rose to his feet and brushed the earth from his knees and fingers. Overhead a bird passed trailing a strange eerie cry.

"The game is getting tighter for me, old friend," he said quietly. "We came so close, Stavros and I, because of you, that I cannot endure waiting any longer. One of these days...one of these days I may strike a solid parlay or run a streak at stud. Then the boy and I will escape. I won't be able to visit you anymore then, but I know you will understand. You know we must go."

He turned and began walking slowly toward the gate. As he crossed the rise of hill he waved back to his friend in a mute gesture of farewell.

There was a night near the end of those two weeks when Matsoukas was awakened by a high shrill scream. The sound shattered his sleep. He stumbled furiously from the bed with Caliope close behind him and ran to the parlor.

Stavros lay rigid within the bed, his cheeks and mouth twisted into the shape of the scream. His eyes stared into space, the pupils wild with fear. His head was thrown back and a terrible gasping for breath bubbled in his throat.

Once again Matsoukas held the heaving body of his son in his arms, suffering each savage wave that ripped the boy's limbs. After the seizure passed he sat watching the boy sleep until dawn split the rim of the night, anguish and fear flaying his flesh.

After that attack, so close to the one the boy had endured before, Matsoukas could not bear to remain away from his son for very long. Sitting at his desk in the office during the morning he would be swept by a violent unrest and would hurry home. He would remain with the boy for hours, playing with him, holding him gently. In those moments he marked the tendons springing from the boy's frame, the meat melting on his arms, the flesh of his cheeks shriveling so all that remained were the boy's great dark eyes. More and more Stavros grew torpid and sluggish, lacking the strength or will to move, lying by the hour on his back, one small-fingered hand twitching slightly in a sign to his father.

There was an afternoon with the sky crusted in a gray low foam when they sat together. Caliope and the girls were out and they were alone except for the mother-in-law brooding in her room. Matsoukas sat on the floor beside the boy's bed, his cheek against the bars, his face just a few inches from his son's head. He saw in that strange moment a yearning in the boy's face, a mute longing, a burning plea for life. He moaned softly and raised his son's hand, pressing the tiny cold fingers to his lips in a fierce caress.

"Lie quietly," Matsoukas said. "Store up your strength. Soon now, I promise you, soon now we will fly." In a cramp of despair he rose to his feet and spread his powerful arms to simulate the wings of a plane. "We will fly," he cried softly. "We will sweep like the wind through the sky!" He moved his arms furiously, wagging them up and down, rumbling through his teeth in imitation of the roar of great engines.

Stavros watched him with a faint light spreading across his face. The tips of his small crooked ears quivered as if they heard the roar of the engines. He gathered the thin bones of his arms, his legs twitched and grew taut, his toes moved in a fin-like flutter.

Matsoukas lowered his arms and crouched once again beside the bed. Stavros curled with a shudder toward his hand.

"Soon now!" Matsoukas cried. He closed his eyes tightly and opened them and smiled at his son. "Soon now, my son, my heart, my soul!"

"What are you mumbling, you fool?" the carp of his mother-in-law swept the room like a vulture's wing. "Why don't you quit tormenting that poor child, trying to make him understand what he cannot ever understand."

Matsoukas sprang to his feet with a snarl.

"You dried-up barracuda!" he said hoarsely. "You wretched old bitch! What do you know? When I talk to him, he understands! He understands every word, every sign!"

She spit at him through the curl of her lips.

"He understands nothing!" she cried shrilly. "He lies there like a vegetable, poor tormented creature, and understands nothing!"

A wild rage shattered his flesh. He reached her in a single great bound and grabbed her by her stringy coarse hair. She let out the howl of a demented witch and coiled her fingers to ward him off.

He locked his hand on the dry hard strands. He evaded her clawing fingers and jèrked her head to one side. Her howl of fury became a shriek of pain. He started to tear loose a clump of her hair when Stavros screamed.

Matsoukas let go the old lady's head and turned to the bed. The boy lay on his side watching them, his eyes open to wide bursting cups, his mouth shaped in the form of a broken shell. One thin arm fluttered in a spasm of terror.

Matsoukas moaned in remorse and ran back to the bed. He raised the boy in his arms, holding him tightly against the shudders that wracked his body. Behind him the old lady gasped hoarsely to regain her breath.

"Bastard!" she spit. "Bastard! God has punished you for your filthy body, for your inhuman soul, for all the debauched evil in your heart!"

He held Stavros close in his arms, rocking him gently, seeking desperately to calm and console him.

"I live for one thing!" the old lady hissed. "I live to see you broken, driven into the sewers where you belong! Animal out of darkness! Bastard and filth is what you are!"

Stavros fluttered his shoulders and Matsoukas softly kissed the boy's trembling cheeks.

"God has punished you with such a son!" the old lady shrieked. "Your filthy seed made him the broken animal he is! You murdered his soul and you'll burn in hell!"

"Soon now, my son," Matsoukas whispered. "Soon we will fly."

"Bastard!" the old lady screamed. "Bastard! Animal! Filth!"

"Soon," Matsoukas said, and he nodded and winked and grimaced at his son. "Soon now, my heart, soon now we will fly."

CHAPTER ELEVEN

THERE was a night he woke with a cry of terror
from a fearful dream. He lay trembling,
sweat erupted across his cold flesh, and his
heart beating like a trapped bird seeking to escape the
cage of his body. For an instant he thought he was dying
and then he caught his breath. Caliope stirred beside him
and raised her head to ask sleepily what was wrong. He
could not answer. After a moment she lowered her head
to the pillow and fell asleep again.

But sleep was strangled that night for him and he lay
in the dark trying to unravel the nightmare. He recalled
that from his open palm a tiny moth had sprung aloft,
sailing into the sky in a swift and jubilant ascent. It was
a dark-winged insect with a butterfly's grace and he
watched it with delight. Higher and higher it rose toward
the corona of the sun. He saw the small wings glimmer
for a moment with a crimson brilliance. A chill swept his
flesh and he cried out a warning but it was too late. A
flash of flame swept the tiny furry body. A puff of smoke
and it blew apart. The soft blackened wings fluttered in
embers and ashes down to the dark sea.

He tried to calm himself. He understood the dream had

been spawned from his growing desperation. Each day his horses continued to run out and he lost steadily at poker. When he won a few dollars it was barely enough to provide him a stake for another hand. He had tried blackjack, roulette, and craps, but these had proved fruitless as well. He was hooked to a deadly losing streak that withered everything he touched. And in that grieving moment the thought of cheating sprang like a demon to birth.

A nausea swept his flesh. He had gambled most of his life, won or lost on his skill and on the diverse elements of chance. He had only contempt for those who sought to alter this balance by swindle and hoax. He swore not to join them.

But in the long slow waning of the night he marked the tremor of his son's frail breathing. He pressed his palms tightly across his ears but the boy's gasps penetrated even that shield. He held his eyes tightly closed and hummed softly under his breath. The hum became a drone and the drone grew in volume until it became a roar. When he took his hands away from his ears the roaring did not cease. It seemed to come from the sky above, the roar of a plane passing overhead, a rumbling that faded slowly. He opened his eyes and saw the first veins of daylight spotted through the fabric of the worn shade. He knew that another flight had left for Greece without them. He made his fearful decision then.

He rose from the bed and went to the bathroom. As he shaved he considered the possibilities. There was no simple way to fix the races so he discarded that prospect. Poker was almost impossible since the dealer controlled the fall of the cards. Blackjack was also dealer-directed and the cards stationary before each player. Only in craps was the player able to control the action. So craps it must be.

When he finished shaving he was conscious that his face had somehow altered. His cheeks seemed sunken as though during the night two long crescent-shaped gashes had been cut into them. There was a hollow darkness to his eyes, a shadow that seeped from the pupil to discolor the iris.

He dressed and left the flat and walked with rapid nervous strides down the street. Inside his office he closed the door and went to his desk to rummage in a bottom drawer. He uttered a deep sigh when he found them, a pair of Busters, crooked dice confiscated from a dice mechanic he had once hurled from a game. They were beautifully made, marvelously balanced, with a series of number combinations that added up to only seven.

All that morning and for the balance of the afternoon he practiced with the dice. He had always had a certain agility in his fingers, and this nimbleness helped him now even as he yearned for Cicero's skill.

For the next three days he repeated the same sequence of movements with the dice. The problem lay in deftly switching the Busters when he was the shooter, then ripping them out of the game and returning the fair dice to play before the next shooter made his throw. To achieve this switch smoothly he practiced with the Busters concealed in his palm and reached for the set of fair dice. He closed his hand, let the Busters drop to his fingers, palmed the fair dice, and threw the Busters for the loaded toss. He depended on the excitement of the game, the tension of the play, to help conceal his switch. At the same time he understood with a feeling of desolation that the greatest possibility of success would result from his unblemished reputation for honest play.

When he finished practicing in the late afternoon he went to Falconis to observe the crap table play in the room which housed the private game. He observed the movement and position of the players, gauging the spot he would wait for, the one on the other side of the table from the door, his right side turned toward the shadows in the corner.

On the morning of the fourth day after his decision he took his passbook to the bank. He withdrew the full amount of their savings balance, two hundred and sixty-two dollars, to use as a stake. He closed the account and endured watching the teller voiding the passbook. From the bank he went downtown to the airline office. He wanted to confirm the reservations for the following morning's flight to Greece. He feared that because of his endless cancellations they would not hold a pair of seats. This time he left a deposit of a hundred dollars, the balance to be paid at the airport before the flight.

He went from there to Falconis'. He stood in a corner of the small back room, watching the crap table action, waiting for the position he had chosen to open. He felt himself trembling, his fingers twitching around the Busters in his pocket, his forehead covered with a strange heavy sweat. Anguish spread cold fingers through his body.

The player holding the position he wanted moved out of the game with a curse. Matsoukas stepped forward to take his place. The player next to him surrendered the dice to Matsoukas for the throw. At the same time he thought with a kind of frenzy of Anthoula.

He was astounded why he had not considered asking her for the money. She told him endlessly how much she adored him. She would understand his great need and aid him.

"I'm out!" he cried and spun away from the table in a surge of excitement.

Outside the Minoan he started at a run for the bakery. By the time he came to the windows laden with sweets and pastries he was almost completely out of breath. He panted around to the alley and knocked urgently on the door. Anthoula opened it.

He stood there with his face flushed, his body shaking, and his breath coming in quick tight gasps. She mistook his disorder for passion and it exploded her own ardor.

"Darling!" she cried hoarsely and pulled him into the kitchen. "You are burning up with love! O my darling!" Desire swept from her body like mist from a marshy bog.

"Listen my dearest," he gasped.

"The old lady is ill today," Anthoula said fervently. "We are alone! O my darling!"

An uneasiness swept him. "Perhaps I should return later," he struggled for breath. "You are busy with the trade."

"Don't move, my darling!" she cried. To prevent him leaving she reached around him and snapped the bolt closed on the door. "Wait!" she cried again and swept to the front of the store. He heard her slam and lock the door and the shade being drawn.

"What will your customers think?" he asked with concern when she flew back. "It is poor business practice to close in the middle of the day."

She did not answer but stretched her arms like pincers

to embrace him, one hand clasping his neck in a vise, the other hand fumbling furiously at the fly of his pants.

"Patience, my beloved!" he gasped in dismay.

She would not release him and tugged him toward the stairs leading to her apartment. She held tightly to his body while uttering soft wild cries of ardor.

"Hurry, my darling!" she moaned. "My nest is on fire!"

"Let me go and we will make it up the stairs more quickly," he tried to speak gaily while struggling vainly to unlock her arm from around his throat.

"I cannot let you go!" she cried. She thrust her knee between his legs so hard he winced.

So they stumbled and bumped the walls and labored up the stairs. Matsoukas cursed silently at her total abandonment of restraint and grace while marveling at her agility. When they reached the second floor he staggered as if they had been humping for hours.

She tugged him toward the bedroom. His fly was open and she endeavored to pull out his organ. He feared if she once got a grip on it she would wrench off the hapless member.

He made it to the bed at the same moment she pulled down his trousers and tore loose two buttons of his shirt. They fell across the spread together and he saw her face swoop down upon him like the beak of some wild bird.

When he finally managed to hold her down long enough to mount her, he ached in every muscle and had to resist a strong impulse to crack her across the snout.

"Take me!" she shrieked. "God, take me!"

He bent in a grim despair to the extension of her body, trying furiously to concentrate, feeling the hard bones of her hips, and the hoard opening and unfolding before his wild numbed thrusts.

Later, lying naked beside her, soaked in an afterglow of exhaustion, he told her about his son and asked her for the money. She screamed. Then she scrambled up to crouch nakedly over him, her great breasts swinging like melons beneath her outraged cheeks.

"You want to leave me!"

"Certainly not!" he protested. "But I have to go!"

"I have given you all my love and now you want to leave me!"

"I love you too, my dearest," he tried to soothe her. "I must go for the sake of my son. He has been ill for a long time and I must take him to Greece."

"Why Greece?" she cried. "The best doctors in the world are here! Why Greece?"

"Not for the doctors," he said slowly. "For the sun of Greece." He shook his head earnestly. "I know it will heal and cure him."

She stared at him with her breath coming in short tight gasps.

"You must be mad!" she cried. "How will the sun cure him of anything? If you are so enamored of sun, take him to Denver for a week!"

He tried patiently to explain again.

"The boy has been ill a long time," he said gently. "The doctors here hold out little hope. They don't understand what the sunlight in Greece is like, the way it reflects off the water. I know . . ."

"Stop talking like a moron!" she cried. She clutched at

him in quick remorse. "The thought of losing you drives me wild!"

"You will not lose me, my darling," he said. "I will continue to love you always."

She shook her head in a mounting frenzy. "I will not let you go! You must not leave me!"

"My darling!" he cried. "You have brought me hours of happiness. You have captured my soul and my heart! I would never leave you now except that my son is ill!"

"You don't love me!"

"I do love you!"

"You don't!"

"I do!" he protested. "I do!"

"If you love me, how can you bear to leave me?"

"I must go!" he cried. "Don't you understand? My son is very ill and I must go!" He felt the helpless tug of his anguish. "If you cannot help me, I must look elsewhere for the money."

He swung his naked legs over the edge of the bed and reached for his underwear on the floor. She threw her arms about his neck in a wild embrace.

He struggled gently to disengage her. As quickly as he loosened her hands, she grabbed him again.

"Don't leave me!" she begged. "Don't leave me, my darling. I will die without you."

He shook his head mutely and managed finally to pull free. "You will not die," he said softly. "You burn with too much life." He bent and pulled his underwear shorts over his legs and up around his naked buttocks. Misery swept his flesh in great waves.

When he turned to pick up his shirt, a seething rage trembled the flesh of her cheeks.

"Go then, goddam you!" she cried.

He made an effort to touch her and she pulled savagely away. "Go, goddam you, go! Don't expect me to be waiting when you come crawling back!"

He looked at her in mute torment.

"I do not expect you to wait for me if you don't wish to wait," he said. "You are free to choose any man you want."

"I will choose ten men!" she laughed hoarsely. "Twenty lovers if I wish! I will find out what real men are like!"

He saw before his eyes the whipping away of love. He balanced wearily on one leg to pull on his trousers.

She leaped naked from the bed and swung her peignoir violently across her shoulders. She held the front tightly overlapping as if suddenly she could not endure being naked before him.

"Do you call yourself a man?" she cried fiercely. "That is a laugh. My dearest husband was ten times more a man than you! He could satisfy me!"

He looked up from tying his shoes, stung by the unfairness of her accusation.

"Perhaps that is why the poor devil is underground," he said.

She waved that aside. "I know you now!" she shouted vengefully. "You are a pervert! You rouse a woman and leave her unsatisfied!"

He started for the door picking up his coat on the way. He looked one final time around the room that he recalled as a nest, a warm and gilded sanctuary. For a bereaved moment he mourned the death of dreams.

"Pervert!" she shrieked. "The arrogance to ask me for

money! I would not give a soiled dime! Pervert! Fairy! Queer!"

He shook his head in wonder before her fury and opened the door leading to the bakery kitchen. "I have loved you and still love you," he said sadly. "I only do what I must do." He paused and sighed. "Pray my beloved, to Zeus," he said slowly. "Pray to Zeus and perhaps he will send you Apollo for no mortal man can fill your insatiable tank."

He started down the stairs rubbing the cold hard dice in his pocket.

Within the back room at Falconis', it was a clockless and hourless night. The light shone hard over the railed table, there were cracks in the boards, and webbed darkness in the corners of the room. The men around the table bent and swayed under the churning and snapping dice. Their thighs bumped, their fingers trembled, and they moved by quick rotation to the toilet to empty their burning bladders.

Matsoukas was ahead about fifty dollars, playing with the fair dice. He waited for his chance to use the Busters, to make three passes in a row doubling his money each time, a hallowed moment when the tension of the game stirred the players to a fever.

An old man cackled the dice in his dry and withered palm. He threw with a brittle snapping motion of his wrist. The dice spit snake eyes. The old man groaned. The dice passed on.

The hands and fingers of the players swept into the beam of light and fleeced and shuffled the dough. A rat-faced man threw a four, gathered the dice and threw again, hurling a missout. The dice passed on.

Matsoukas made small and medium wagers, winning a few dollars with the fair dice, playing cautiously, girding for his big throw. He kept a wary eye on the house man who drifted around the table tabbing the game. He felt the Busters in his pocket weighing down his clothing. He made a hasty trip into the foul toilet to stand over the bowl stinking of urine and desperation.

He returned to the table and played for another hour. He knew he could not delay ripping in the Busters much longer without becoming sick. A dark hot bile kept bubbling in his belly. With his fingers shaking he counted his money into two neat piles, one of seventy-five dollars and the other of a hundred and twenty-five dollars. He reached slowly in his pocket and palmed the Busters. When the dice reached him he shoved in the larger amount of the money and withdrew his hand from his pocket. He picked up the fair dice and deftly switched them with the Busters in his palm.

"I am all out for action!" he cried. "My hundred-twenty-five bucks of front money begs to be doubled! Come on and fade Matsoukas!"

When he was covered he raised his hand and felt a wild quiver down his back. Each movement of his arm seemed an incalculable burden. He threw the Busters with a groan. The four and trey snapped up in response. His heart gave a jump and he reached quickly for the dice.

"Two-hundred and fifty stays," he cried. "Keep your pretzels and peanuts in your pockets! Raise your pokes and fade my bet!"

Once more he was covered and once more with wild abandon he threw. The seven clicked up again.

"One more time!" Matsoukas cried. "Are you high rollers or squips? Don't squawk when you crap out! This game is a steeplechase and I have five hundred hurdles!"

He picked up the dice and rattled them in his fingers waiting for his money to be faded. He felt as though his heart were a worm, stirring beneath a rock. He threw the Busters, saw them whirl and blur, strike the rail, hurl off to churn to a stop. The third natural made several men curse. A sigh swept like wind through his body and he reached quickly for the money and the dice, the fair dice waiting to be switched in his palm. He pushed in the second pile of money containing seventy-five dollars. He would rip the Busters out, throw fair, and quit.

Suddenly two of the men across the table from Matsoukas were shoved aside. The cold twisted face of the Turk, Youssouf, appeared between them. His big hairy hand reached down to snap up the Busters. Matsoukas cried out and felt his breath twist like a knife up his throat.

Youssouf grinned at Matsoukas and bent forward slightly to come under the light. He examined the dice. A weird tuneless hiss broke from his lips. "Get Falconis!" he said harshly to a man at the table. The man scurried off. The Turk looked at Matsoukas.

Matsoukas felt the moment black and long, coiled like a serpent about his head. The players at the table looked from Youssouf to him. And shame carved a wound in his flesh.

He heard the door open and Falconis appeared at the table, his face pale and tense. The Turk motioned toward

Matsoukas and then rattled the dice in his hand. With a droll and voracious grin he hurled them across the table. The four and three snapped up again.

"Busters!" the Turk cried fiercely. "The whoreson Greek using Busters!"

An angry hiss and mutter broke from the players around the table. One man cursed furiously, another shoved Matsoukas from behind, and a third man spit at him. A trickle of the saliva dripped down his cheek.

"Matsoukas! Matsoukas!" Falconis said in a horrified voice. "How could you do such a thing?"

Matsoukas tried to muster a defense. The words died in a futile little moan at his lips. He slowly pushed the money he had won to the center of the table to be apportioned among the players. He looked back silently at the distraught Falconis.

"Get out, Matsoukas!" Falconis cried shrilly. "Never come back in here again for any play! I erase the cursed debt you owe me! I want nothing from an animal like you except never to set eyes on you again!"

Youssouf made an angry sweep with his arm and caught the owner's shoulder in a wild hard grip.

"Goddam, no!" he said fiercely.

"I have forbidden him ever to return," Falconis said helplessly. "He will never be able to play in any gambling house again. That is his punishment."

"Goddam, no!" Youssouf cried and the veins in his neck swelled with blood. "Goddam, no! I have waited too long for this moment!"

Falconis looked trembling at the Turk. The men around the table grew still. Falconis tried to speak again but terror had muted his tongue. He stared at Matsoukas in despair.

"Let the gorilla try," Matsoukas said, and his voice did not seem his own, the words born of a strange and weary lament. "I have it coming and he has the right to try."

He turned toward the alcove and walked out the door. He moved down the narrow hall leading to the basement. He felt his body suspended between resignation and despair. He heard the Turk coming behind him.

They faced each other in the shadowed basement, a single large low-ceilinged room bricked on all sides except for the door through which they had entered. No sound from the world above penetrated here, and no cry of torment or pain could be heard in any of the rooms upstairs. It was an anteroom of Hades, the only light a single yellow bulb swinging in a metal shade.

Matsoukas untied his shoes and kicked them off to one side. He took off his jacket and loosened and removed his tie. Youssouf had stripped to the waist and his great muscled arms and powerful shoulders were smeared with the same green heavy oil that glistened on his bald boar's head. His huge bare toes clung webbed to the dirt floor.

They began warily to circle one another. Matsoukas flexed his arms but could not shake the lassitude, the weakness that foraged through his body.

The Turk lashed a searing kick at his groin. Matsoukas leaped aside barely evading the hard cutting toes.

They came slowly together again. The Turk charged with a grunt and Matsoukas spun away and landed a wild chop across the Turk's neck, feeling the huge boned head quiver, a small spit of air hiss from his lips. At arms length they jabbed and chopped, stiff fingers and knuckles stabbing for nerve centers of soft flesh.

Youssouf charged again trying to drive Matsoukas against the wall. Matsoukas held him off with a savage flurry of blows that stopped his advance and yet could not drive him back. Their bodies rammed together, their fingers flailing to lock one another's arms, freezing their limbs in a wild clawed grip.

Matsoukas strained and heaved for an edge, blood bursting through his veins. He cried out fiercely seeking the fire and power in his body, but his flesh quivered weakly and would not respond. His bones creaked and bent to snap. He felt his spirit wavering, his strength falling away like fragments broken from a piece of crushed rock. A tearing despair leaped through his loins and he felt the Turk gaining. Even as he was driven to his knees, his arms torn aside, he felt his heart surrender like a corpse.

The Turk beat him down with a wild rocking blow. His head shuddered and fingers of shock stabbed through his temples. He tried to rise from his knees and the Turk struck him again. His senses fled shrieking. He swayed and waited with pain plummeting through his body to his testicles. A frantic thread of spittle, slow and thick as honey, ran from the corner of his mouth.

Another terrible blow burst in his throat. He felt the spurt of his blood, teeth shattered in his mouth. His agony passed into numbness and he felt himself in a sea of foaming billows.

He huddled palsied and shattered and through his terror saw the enraged Turk's foot rise and arc and he could not move to avoid it. The ridge of toes caught his cheek, split the flesh, one toe gouging the soft pulp of his eye. A flame burst in his head and he felt himself falling. His cheek struck the cold damp earth and he burrowed in it like a mole. He tasted kinship in that moment to an animal being slaughtered. The yellow lamp shone down with a cold and unblinking light. And with a sudden strange calm he knew that the Turk was going to kill him.

He watched him approach. He could see the high broad ridges of the Turk's body, crags of rock and clumps of brush. The Turk crouched beside him and caught him by the hair. His head was yanked off the dirt and the Turk's arm coiled around his throat to strangle off the air that held him to life.

"Let me live," Matsoukas whispered.

The Turk paused and bent closer to hear.

"Let me live," Matsoukas pleaded, and the words bubbled from his bloodied lips. "For the sake of my son."

Youssouf wavered. His arm continued to lock and press but the fingers trembled. His breath came in short hoarse gasps and the scent of oil and sweat and hate raged suddenly in a fearful struggle against something within him. Matsoukas hung in the thunder of each heartbeat. Then Youssouf moaned and released him, thrusting his head back to the dirt. The Turk swung off his heels and rose to his feet and stepped away. And Matsoukas heard his soul cry out.

CHAPTER TWELVE

HE entered their flat and moved slowly from the hall into the parlor. The light from the windows shredded the bars of his son's bed, cutting strips of shadow and moonglow across his small blanket-covered body.

He gripped the bars and lowered himself painfully to the floor. His body ached fearfully, riots of pain razing his flesh. The socket of his wounded eye flicked with fire. He felt a segment of the torn lid congealed with blood so it would not close but remained hinged apart.

He heard steps from the bedroom and after a moment Caliope came up beside him.

"You're early," she said. "It's not daylight yet."

He wanted to tell her to return to bed but he could not assemble the words. If he opened his mouth he feared he would cry out.

"Be careful you don't wake him," she said "He was restless all evening."

She came closer and he turned his face away. She seemed to sense that something was wrong. He motioned her aside with a gesture of his hand.

The moon emerged from behind a cloud and shone

through the windows. He felt her hand on his shoulder, tugging his body around. For an instant he fought her and then resigned himself. He turned his face to the light and stared up at her seeing her cheeks a blurred oval suspended against the shadow and mist of the room.

She drew her breath in sharply. He looked back toward the sleeping figure of his son.

"What happened?" she whispered. "In the name of God, what happened to you?"

"I fought the Turk," he said slowly.

"Why?"

He thought of rising and fleeing but his arms and legs were a ponderous burden that he could not lift.

"Why?" she asked again.

He imagined her watching him, the black cold hollows about her eyes.

"I cheated," he said, and the words burned his tongue. "I cheated."

There was a moment of stunned silence and then she laughed. Yet it was not really laughter because there was no mirth in her voice, only a savage expelling of air.

"Not you!" she said mockingly and he felt the naked glitter of her eyes. "Not you with your uncompromising virtue, your lofty sense of honor, your consecrated ethics at gambling. Not you!"

He did not answer. He put his finger to the socket of his eye and felt the torn lid shoot sparks of pain through his body.

She moved from the bed. She walked to one of the windows and stood for a moment with her back to him. The curtain stirred before her, a ripple of wind passing down the filmy cloth. She turned and came back to loom dark and vengefully above him.

"Are you becoming human then?" she asked. "Are you beginning finally to walk the earth with us poor mortals? Are you starting to understand the weaknesses of our flesh?"

He felt the first stirring of cold wind from a forest of black cypresses, a wind carrying the chill of damp blossoms and wet soil. He leaned forward wearily and rested his cheek against the bars of the bed.

"Ten years," she said and he trembled at the fury rising from the marrow of her bones, "Ten years of living with you, sleeping with you, watching you indulge in the absurd ritual of your days and nights. You lodged in some place of rarefied air where only Matsoukas could breathe, a land denied the ordinary slob."

Stavros fluttered his fingers on the pillow and Matsoukas reached between the bars and drew the corner of the blanket gently over his hand.

"God, why did I marry you? Why of all the women in the world you might have graced with your studding virtues and your incomparable temperament did it have to be me? What screw of chance decided that stroke?"

He tried to close his eyes but the torn lid would not shut. The eye stared unblinking at the pale glimmer of moonlight through the curtains.

"If you knew how much I hated you," she whispered. "O God, I think hate has kept me alive. Even when I lie beneath your heaving loins with your matchless cock buried in my body, even then I think my hate is most of the passion and I wish my body were a great claw to draw you into me and devour you, destroy you."

173

A vision of her face in their moments of love came to him. He recalled the large luminous glitter of her eyes and a shudder swept his body.

"But I was not always that way," she said and for an instant her voice wavered. "I loved you when we married. I thought you were full of grace and strength. I did not know then you would move through life like a bird scattering shit where you wished, keeping yourself untouched, unblemished, unsoiled."

He felt her words hooking his flesh, gouging his wounds, probing for his soul.

"Even the boy, God help him, was always yours," she said. "He was your son. Only your love could save him and nourish him. I was only his mother, only the woman who held him inside her body for the months before his birth, only the woman who brought him into the world in a tide of blood and bile. When they washed him off, cleansed his body of the slime, then he was your son."

The words hissed from her mouth, sharpened and flung from the taut tendons of her rage.

"I think sometimes you were to blame! I think you believed he was the son of a God and the Gods you revere as your relations decided to smite your arrogance. They covered him with a cloud to punish you, a madman, a bastard, a fool!"

He moved his trembling hand and the soft strands of the boy's hair slipped beneath his fingers. The scalp was warm. He touched it lightly, embracing the delicate crown.

"And right to the end you indulge your absurd dreams," she said. "You tear about like a maddened animal, an insane fool seeking to carry a dying son to some land of dreams. You are mad and this dream is the maddest one of all, this dream of flight with a dying child."

He shook his head. The light beyond the window swayed again. He wanted to cry out but he could not speak.

"He is dying, Matsoukas," she said, and for the first time he heard clearly the cry of her anguish. "The boy is dying. Whether here or in Greece, he will die soon. Not even you can avert that. He is dying and no power on earth can save him from that death."

"No," he said, and the word came torn from his lips. "No."

"Yes!" she said, "Goddam you, yes! Accept that truth and there might be hope for you to join the mortals. He is dying. He will die soon. Flight is useless."

"No," he said helplessly. "No."

"Yes! Yes! Yes!" she cried. She came closer and he tensed waiting for her to strike him. "Bastard! Madman! Fool! Yes! Yes! Yes!"

A weird moan sounded in his ears. It was a moment before he understood that it came from him. He felt it gathering like a wave within his body, swelling to crest past his lungs and his heart, rising through his throat, bursting from the scar of his lips. Again and again it rose and each time the wild stricken moan broke free.

He felt Caliope's hands pulling him to his feet. She led him from the parlor down the hall to the bathroom. She snapped on the light. His torn eye burned beneath the glare.

He stood mute and unmoving while she washed him.

He felt her fingers, the warm wet cloth soaking his bruises, softly wiping away the crusts of dried blood, dabbing the sore gums from which several of his teeth had been driven. She patted his cheek with cotton pads of peroxide and covered the torn lid and socket of his eye with a square of gauze that she taped to his temple and the bridge of his nose. When she finished, as if he were a child, she ran a brush through his thick tangled hair. He saw then with a strange shaken distress that she was crying.

She left the bathroom and he stood for a moment uncertain where to go. He walked back up the hall to the parlor. He bent once more over his son's bed, reaching out his hand to touch him, trying to console his anguish in the feel of the boy's flesh.

He heard Caliope return. She came to stand beside him at the bed. He saw her face filled now with a cold hard strength.

"Raise the boy and take him," she said, and the words came quick and sharp. "I have packed his clothing and shirts and trousers for you. I will give you blankets to wrap around him. You can catch a taxi for the airport on the boulevard."

He stared at her numbly, uncomprehending.

"Will you move!" she cried softly. She thrust her clenched fist toward him. "Here is the money for your tickets, enough besides to house and feed you both for a while. Hurry now!"

For a grieving moment he thought she had impaled him with a barbarous jest. But in the light from the hall he saw the sheaf of wrinkled bills in her fingers.

She shook her head, savagely rejecting his questions,

motioning to him to raise Stavros. At that instant a wild shriek of betrayal rang through the flat, a fearful scream of loss from her mother's room.

"Hurry!" Caliope cried. "I have locked her in! Go now before she wakes the dead!"

Then everything was swept aside in his frenzy to flee. He stuffed the money into his wallet. He held the boy in his arms while Caliope wrapped the blankets tightly around him, folding the corners about his head to shield his face. He moved to the suitcase by the door and remembered his daughters. He made a mute appeal to Caliope and carrying Stavros, hurried down the hall to their room. As he passed the old lady's room she began to beat with her bony fists against the wood of the door.

He bent over his sleeping daughters, seeing their blonde and lovely faces serene and untroubled. He tenderly kissed each little girl farewell.

He hurried back to the hall where Caliope waited with the suitcase by the door. He wavered, looking toward the old lady's room, hearing her crazed howls.

"I can handle her," Caliope said. "She will not let us starve. It will be no worse than before."

He moved to open the door and Stavros stirred in his arms.

"Wait!" Caliope cried. He turned back and she reached out slowly and pulled aside the blanket covering her son's face. She bent and for a long moment kissed the boy's lips. When she rose, she turned away so Matsoukas could not see her face.

He stared at her back and was afraid to touch her or to speak. He turned then, picked up the suitcase, and holding Stavros tightly in his arms, he fled down the stairs.

With their tickets secure in his pocket he sat in the huge airport terminal, in one of the armchairs before the great glass windows that ran from the ceiling to the floor. Beyond the windows the moon was gone and the night was charcoal-black.

He carried Stavros in his arms. The boy's face was visible within the folds of blanket, and in the cold gray terminal light, his cheeks were the bleak shade of a tomb. His fingers, like small brittle twigs, hung stiffly close to his lips. He slept in a strange deep slumber.

Now, in the hour of their departure, Matsoukas could feel no jubilation. He endured only a resignation and despair. He pressed his cheek against the folds of the blanket. He rested and heard the heavy slow beating of his heart. The sounds of the terminal, the loudspeaker announcing flights, faded to a drone.

When he raised his head again there had been a shift in the night, the charcoal-blackness screened to the shade of putty. He could sense a faint stirring in the earth, areas of mist shepherded, trees emerging dimly from the pitch. Even as he watched, a series of dark and gray hillocks sprang from the ground.

Their flight was announced and he rose with Stavros to walk to the gate. Raw pain and weariness spliced together in his body.

He moved from the main terminal under an archway and down a long corridor. In each alcove he passed, the long windows showed the altering sky, a partition of the shades of darkness and light, a slow veiling of the stars.

He had never before seen so clearly the ritual of the dawn. The first faint light like a dry and clean host assaulting the minions of darkness. A quiver swept his flesh.

When he reached the gate to their plane he stood with Stavros before the windows looking out across the field. The huge formless shape of their plane was still hinged to the darkness around the terminal.

Then the light, slowly, ravenously, gained dominance. Shreds of nightclouds, swarthy and grimed, were plucked like struggling chickens and silently butchered. The dark grays and deep purples gave way to faint blues. And far out at the edge of the earth, no more than a frail orange glow on the horizon, he saw the first trace of the sun.

His breath caught sharply in his throat. He raised Stavros high in his arms so that the blanket fell away. The breaking dawn swept the boy's dark cheeks with a flickering warmth. He stirred and opened his eyes.

The corona of the sun ascended. Matsoukas stretched out his hand and felt the burnished glow soothe his palm and fingers. A wild excitement tore his body.

And then the head, the lustrous scorching head of the sun broke over the curve of the earth. The last shadows hurled away, the final dull patches of night fled screaming. Like a fierce firebird the sun swooped. It rubied the fuselages of planes, crimsoned the runways and hangars, incarmined the conclave of buildings, reddened the spirals of the tower. It blazed across their plane. The wings flushed scarlet, swelling suddenly with a gleaming and fearful power.

The sun burst across the window where they stood, a radiance like a thousand rainbows streaming through the glass, sealing Stavros and himself in a blazing glitter.

Their flight was boarding and he hurried to the tunnel. Through the seams and folds of the bellows, he still felt the sun, fetal and molten, spinning and whirling through his blood.

His heart cried out. He felt the tears burst from his eyes, fitfully from the torn lid, jubilant and grateful tears. They fell in specks of flame upon the blanket of his son.

In this way, crying and holding Stavros tightly in his arms, he boarded the wild-winged plane.

CPSIA information can be obtained
at www.ICGtesting.com
Printed in the USA
FFOW04n1455250615
14618FF